FUR THE HEX OF IT

THE GRAVESTONE MYSTERIES - BOOK ONE

JANE HINCHEY

BAYWOLF PRESS

BP

BAYWOLF PRESS

This is for you…
If this book lifts you up, if it helps you take a break from reality and takes you away from your troubles if only for a moment… then I've done my job.

xoxo
Jane

Holly Day isn't who she thinks she is.

Forced into hiding in the small town of Gravestone, she's under strict instructions not to use her magic. If only it were that easy.

When her rat familiar unearths a human bone—in Holly's backyard—she's on the case. Only Holly has another problem... her memory is like swiss cheese—full of holes. Is she really the SIA Agent she thinks she is? Or is something more sinister at play?

Trying to keep a low profile and stay under the radar of the local police is easier said than done when she teams up with super senior, Doris Shutt, the pair of them determined to get to the bottom of the mysterious bone before the Sheriff throws Holly in jail, for good.

CHAPTER
One

Dust billowed in the air, coating me in a fine layer of grit, sticking to my skin and making my nose twitch. I stepped onto the median, away from the rumbling old bus that had dropped me off, and now wheezed and backfired as it pulled away, gravel spitting from beneath its tires.

"Well, Flynn," I said to the rat who sat on my shoulder. "What do you think?"

We looked at the faded town sign where we'd been deposited. Gravestone. Population eight hundred and fifty-nine. How the Supernatural Investigation Agency had found this place, I didn't know, and as much as I disliked the very idea of laying low, Gravestone was to be my new home. For now, at least. The SIA had fabricated a backstory that I was a long-lost relative of recently deceased John Smith and had come to claim my inheritance, such as it was.

The summer sun beat down on us. Despite it being

not yet noon, the heat of the day was almost unbearable, and Flynn tunneled his way under my hair, seeking shade.

"I hear ya," I muttered, already feeling my skin prickle and sweat start to pool in places I'd rather not think about. Sliding my sunglasses up my nose, I grabbed the handle of my suitcase and pulled it along behind me as we made our way down the pothole-littered road into the township of Gravestone itself. My left foot was encased in an orthopedic walking boot up to my knee, making progress slow. Yet, despite my apparent injury, the bus driver refused to enter the town, electing to drop me off at the outskirts to shave a few precious minutes off his route.

I'd been sorely tempted to zap his butt with a blast of magic, but Flynn had been quick to nix that idea with a lick to the side of my neck in warning. It was all I could do not to fling him off me in revulsion. *Gross.* But he'd not only seen my fingers flex, he'd also felt the power surge of magic vibrating beneath my skin, preparing to erupt. Which was partly why Flynn was with me today. As my ex-partner, he was finely attuned to my magic, and, according to my boss, I was not to use my magic while residing in Gravestone. In fact, I was to keep my witch status under lock and key altogether. Hence the swift response from Flynn. No magic. At all. Full stop. Basically, I was to pretend I was human, and to be perfectly honest, despite my exemplary skills as an undercover SIA agent, I had a niggling worry I had finally met my match and was on a case I couldn't pull off.

Flynn was a prime example that things could, and sometimes did, go wrong. Flynn was, in fact, Gavin Flynn, shifter and fellow SIA Agent, only he'd copped the brunt of the blast that had taken us down. Now he was a rat, and I had a broken foot. Somehow, I thought I got the better deal. Except I was saddled with him as my *familiar*. Honestly, I didn't think my boss, Scott Harding, knew what to do with him, so handing him off to me was the easiest option.

Grumbling beneath my breath, I continued the trek toward town, cursing the fact I didn't have a hat or sunscreen as the sun's rays beat down on us, unrelenting in their goal of frying me to a crisp. My foot started to twinge, and my limp became more pronounced the farther we walked. Right now, I'd kill for water. Beer would be better. After all, I was on an enforced vacation, may as well kick back, relax, and enjoy a few adult beverages. The only problem? I didn't know how to kick back or relax. But Harding had convinced me I needed to at least press pause if I wanted to come out of this alive.

On my last assignment, I'd had the good fortune—or was it misfortune—to stumble upon a wand smuggling ring. Not only were the wands counterfeit, but they were also tainted with dark magic. Deadly magic. The wands had been weaponized. I'd grabbed one as proof, and to try and find where they were manufactured, when I'd been spotted and my cover blown. Harding had me extracted, and I'd handed over the wand and all the intel I'd gathered. Only the safe house he'd temporarily stashed me in had been compromised, an attack launched in the dead of night. Flynn, who'd been assigned as my bodyguard, was the one who woke me in time for us to escape, but we'd been caught in a magical blast that had changed both our lives irrecoverably. Now, Harding suspected the SIA had a mole—and I had a price on my head. Oh, and Flynn was turned into a rat.

So, here I am, sweating up a storm in Gravestone, suitcase, walking boot, and pet rat in tow, although every time I referred to Flynn as my pet, he'd bite me. So touchy.

"I need to rest," I said through gritted teeth, shoving the extendable handle of my suitcase down and balancing my butt on the top of said suitcase, taking the weight off my leg. SIA medics couldn't heal me or return Flynn to his usual form. But they didn't know what I knew. We'd been hit by one of the counterfeit wands. Dark magic. The break in my foot would eventually heal on its own, but I had to wear the walking boot and learn patience until then. Patience had never been my strong suit. I wondered if Flynn would regain his human form in time as well, or if he was stuck in this furry, four-legged state forever.

I heard the car approaching before I saw it. The cloud of dust was a dead giveaway as well. Sitting on my suitcase by the side of the road, I reached a hand up to Flynn, who was peeking out around the curve of my neck, most likely wondering what fresh hell I'd gotten us into, when a sheriff's truck shot past, hit the brakes, and skidded around in a U-turn before pulling to a halt beside me. Burying my face in the crook of my arm, I waited for the dust cloud to settle, all the while cursing Gravestone and its poor excuse for a road.

"Excuse me, ma'am, is everything okay?"

Lowering my arm, I looked up at the man behind the wheel. His elbow rested on the door, window down, as he looked me over, his lips curling in a slow, sexy smile.

"Oh, everything is just dandy," I snapped, my mood soured by the heat, dust, and unconscionably long trek from the main road to town. I should have insisted the driver do his actual job and deposit me in town. Preferably right at my doorstep. But I hadn't known then what I knew now—that it was one hell of a walk. "I figured it was a beautiful day for a walk." Sarcasm dripped from every word, and Flynn ducked beneath my hair, recognizing the tone and knowing I was not in the mood to be trifled with. Bad enough that I'd been forced into hiding, but to be sent here, the ass-end of nowhere, was insult to injury.

The sexy smile slipped. "What's your name?"

"What's yours?"

"Sheriff Joshua Calder," he introduced himself. "Protecting the citizens of Gravestone."

"Protecting them from what? Boredom?"

His brows shot up. "All right then," he said, removing his elbow from the window frame and wrapping his fingers around the steering wheel. "I see you've got this all under control." He'd shoved the truck in gear and prepared to leave when common sense smacked me in the face.

"Wait!" I yelled.

He paused and turned his head to look at me, saying nothing, engine idling.

Through gritted teeth, I said, "If it's not too much trouble, I'd appreciate a lift. I didn't realize it was so far when the bus dropped me off."

Sheriff Calder's eyes widened. "Hector dropped you off?"

"If Hector is the old as dirt driver who smells like pine tree air freshener, then yes, Hector dropped me off."

Sheriff Calder shook his head, turned off the engine, and climbed out of his truck. "He should know better," he muttered under his breath. "Here, let me help you with that." He moved to take the suitcase, but I extended the handle and kept a firm hold on it.

"I can manage."

"I'm sure you can. Excuse me for being polite." His sarcasm matched my own. The last thing I needed was to get on the radar of local law enforcement, so, swallowing my pride, I released the handle. "By all means." I left him to it and hobbled my way around the truck to the passenger door. Truth be told, I was grateful for the lift.

Two minutes later, we were driving down the pothole-riddled road.

"So, what brings you to Gravestone?" the sheriff asked. "Vacation?" The hopeful inflection in his voice was impossible to miss. No doubt wishing that I was here for a short time, and he'd be putting me in the rearview sooner rather than later. I get that a lot.

"Inheritance." It was time to bust out my cover story. "My great uncle passed away recently."

He frowned. "Your great uncle? The only person who's passed recently was old John Smith, and he had no relatives."

"Correction. He was my mother's estranged uncle."

"Are you sure?"

"I'm here, aren't I?" I ground out. I rummaged in my bag for my pain killers, shaking two into my palm before tossing them into my mouth.

I could feel his eyes on me. "Hurts, huh?" The walking boot was relatively well hidden by the long flowing skirt I wore, which was another part of my undercover assignment. Wear dresses. Fit in. I was not a dress girl, although I had to say that I was rather grateful for the cool cotton this particular garment offered in the heat.

"What tipped you off?" *Oh my God, would you just stop already!* The poor sheriff had done nothing wrong. I didn't know why all I was giving him was grief. Which was a lie in itself. I was in a foul mood because I was off the case, to put it in a nutshell. I was benched. I was in hiding. And it rankled like a burr under my saddle.

He looked at me for a second longer, mouth compressed into a line so thin his lips practically disappeared. Yep. Pissed him off. Well done, Holly. Five minutes into your new life, and you're already on the wrong side of local law enforcement. A record.

Flynn chose that exact moment to peep his head out from beneath my hair, his whiskers twitching as he stood on his hind legs and leaned toward the sheriff, sniffing.

"Oh my God, what is that?" The truck swerved and bounced into a pothole, throwing me against the door. My head smacked on the side window with an audible crack before he regained control and quickly apologized.

I reached up and grabbed Flynn, cradling him in my hands. "This is Flynn. My pet rat." Flynn restrained from biting me but shot me a look that said he wasn't pleased at the pet reference. Too bad.

"Urgh!" He shivered. "Who keeps a rat as a pet?"

"I do." My voice dripped ice, and Flynn's tail swished across my wrist. I wasn't sure if he was soothing me or joining me in my irritation.

"Well, keep it away from me. I don't like rodents." The sheriff's shudder was totally uncalled for.

"Suits me." I stroked my hand down Flynn's back, his fur as soft as a kitten's, then tucked him back up on my shoulder. Flynn immediately made himself invisible, hiding beneath the heavy curtain of my hair.

We continued the drive in silence while I overtly studied Sheriff Joshua Calder. Early forties. Tall. Fit. A sprinkling of salt and pepper at the temples. Laugh lines indicated he did smile on occasion. Carried himself with an air of confidence, suggesting he'd been sheriff of Gravestone for some time and was comfortable in his role.

"The road is being re-sealed next week," he said into the silence, making me jump.

"Right."

"It's not always this bad," he continued, as if embarrassed about the state of the road. "The whole thing has been a pain in my rear from start to finish. Rather than laying asphalt on top, the mayor wanted the old road dug up."

"Right."

"That took a week."

Given the machinery we have available for such tasks, that seemed an extraordinary amount of time. "What were they using, oxen?"

"Might as well have been." His sigh was heartfelt, and my earlier animosity eased a fraction. I understood frustration. "Then a storm hit."

"Hence the potholes."

"Hence the potholes," he agreed. "Next week can't come quick enough. Three cars have already lost their mufflers, driving like maniacs."

"Is that why you were out this way? Patrolling for maniacs?" I knew what was coming as soon as the words had left my mouth.

"Have I found one?"

"Har har."

We pulled up outside what could only be described as a ruin. John Smith's house was in a state of disrepair, to put it mildly. A strong gust of wind could blow the whole thing over any second.

"You have got to be kidding me," I said under my breath, gazing at the atrocity from the safety of Sheriff Jacob Calder's truck.

He kept the engine idling, rested one arm on top of the steering wheel, and joined me in studying my new home. "Needs a little work."

"You don't say." The sarcasm was back.

"I could drop you at Joan Jackson's B&B if you'd prefer," he offered. "It's closer to town. And cleaner."

While his offer was tempting, I had strict orders. Harding needed to know where I was, which was here, number one Berryman Street, Gravestone. Staying at paid accommodations led to complications like money trails and official records. I'd had to hand over my SIA-issued phone and badge and grudgingly accept the burner phone Harding handed me. His last words to me had been, "I don't care how awful it is. I don't care if you hate it. Suck it up. You're staying at John Smith's house on the pretense he is your great uncle. Understood?"

"Yes, sir!"

I turned to the sheriff and did my best to smile. My face practically cracked. Had it been that long since I'd smiled? The muscles felt odd, frozen, as if they didn't know what to do with this strange expression I was inflicting upon them. "I'll be fine here."

Opening the door, I slid out of the truck, taking a moment to get my balance. The sheriff shut off the engine and walked to the back of his truck, hauling my suitcase out and bringing it around to where I stood at the front gate. Or rather, where the front gate would be if it were standing. I spotted a few slats of wood rotting in the weeds to my right and assumed once upon a time they'd stood sentinel at the entry of the property.

"John's place backs up to the mangroves," the sheriff said. "Just in case you hear any unfamiliar sounds."

I cocked my head and studied him. "Anything I should be worried about?" I knew nothing about mangroves or what types of critters lived in them.

"Not you. But you might want to keep your friend inside. He'd make a tasty snack for some of the wildlife."

Flynn's claws dug into my skin. Yeah, I'd be

concerned too if, instead of the hunter, I was the prey. I felt a trickle of sweat roll down the side of my face and wiped it away. "Thanks for the lift," I said, taking the suitcase from him. "Guess I should let you get back to patrolling for maniacs."

He inclined his head. "Welcome to Gravestone."

I waited until he'd climbed back into his truck and driven away before proceeding down the cracked concrete path, admiring the tenacity of the weeds that had forced themselves up through the cracks and were thriving in their barren landscape. Two steps led to a buckled porch, and the wooden slats groaned in protest as I walked across them. I stood for a moment, studying them. "You know, Flynn, we could probably do something with this. I've got time on my hands. We could turn this into a fixer-upper project. How are you with a hammer?"

Flynn rubbed his face against my jaw, then licked me, making me flinch. "What did I say about licking me? Only when you're alerting me to something. I don't care if you like the taste of my sweat. It's just gross, so cut it out." I lifted him off my shoulder and cradled him in my hand while I wrestled with the front door. Harding had handed me an envelope along with the burner phone. In it had been my new identity and the keys to this place. Tess Hunter, Twitch to her friends, was gone. In her place, Holly Day, bookstore clerk. Harding had thought my new name was hilarious, and I knew why he'd left it until the last minute to tell me. So that I couldn't do anything about it.

"Remember, Twitch," he'd said somberly, hands on my shoulders and peering into my face. I'd never seen him so earnest. "This is life and death. You stumbled onto something big, and until we get to the bottom of it, you're not safe. I need you to stay in Gravestone. Become Holly. Do not reveal to anyone, under any circumstances, that you are Twitch the Witch."

His voice echoed in my head as if he was standing right next to me. The hairs on the back of my neck stood on end, and I swiveled, eyes scanning the weed-filled front garden and beyond. Nothing. No one was about. No one was watching. Just the hum of bees and the distant call of birds in the trees. Yet I had the eerie sensation I was not alone.

There were two houses on Berryman Street. John Smith's was one of them, which actually made it perfect. Only one neighbor to worry about. Were they watching me now? Can't say I'd blame them. If our roles were reversed, that's exactly what I'd do—have my nose pressed against the glass checking out the new neighbor.

"Come on, Flynn, let's get inside. I think the heat is getting to me." Propping the screen door open with my foot, I inserted the key into the weathered wooden door, and with a bit of brute force, the key turned in the lock. Putting my shoulder to the door, I pushed hard, then stumbled inside when it gave way beneath my weight. Dust motes danced in the air as our entrance stirred the only breeze the house had seen in weeks. Setting Flynn on the floor, I dragged my suitcase inside and closed the screen door, leaving the wooden door open to try to air the place out. I felt like I'd walked into a dusty oven, the heat inside the closed-up house as unrelenting as the heat outside.

The living room consisted of a worn, stained armchair, a torn-up sofa, a coffee table laden with old newspapers and empty beer cans, an overflowing ashtray, and the oldest television I'd ever seen. A thick layer of dust coated everything, making me sneeze. "What have you gotten me into, Harding?" It was a rhetorical question. As far as hiding places went, I couldn't fault him. Who would think to look for me here, a tiny coastal town in South Texas that barely registered on the map, in a run-down cottage that would probably only sell for land value and very little else?

This was not your standard SIA safe house. Not by a long shot. But these weren't your average circumstances either. Harding had hidden me here off the books. He feared there was a mole in the SIA. Otherwise, how had they known where to find me? The safe house I'd initially been placed in should have been that. Safe. Yet they'd found me and had almost succeeded in killing me. And that had Harding rattled. Since I had enough self-preservation not to want to be dead, I'd deemed it more than appropriate to follow Harding's instructions.

"No point dwelling on it, eh, Flynn? It is what it is, and I may as well just get on with it. First things first, let's clean up a bit. And for the love of God, get off that armchair! I don't know what that stain is, but I'm thinking maybe old John Smith died in that chair."

Flynn twitched his whiskers and ignored me. Of course, he'd love the smell of decomposition. He was a rat. Didn't matter that he used to be human. Well, not human exactly, a shifter. But now that he was a rat, he'd taken on all rat characteristics, which was kinda unnerving.

The hours ticked by surprisingly fast. After throwing open the doors and windows, I'd hauled my suitcase upstairs, vetoing the main bedroom for the much smaller second bedroom at the back of the house. No way was I sleeping on the double bed currently occupying John's room. I didn't know what happened to the old man but to say he wasn't big on hygiene was an understatement. I was going to need cleaning supplies, stat.

"Yoohoo! Anybody home?" The banging on the front door was insistent, and I suspected whoever the voice belonged to knew I was here and had no intention of leaving until I answered their summons. Dropping the garbage bag I'd been dragging around the living room, I appeared in the doorway.

"Yes?" I knew I looked a mess. I could feel it in my very bones. Drenched in sweat, covered in dust, no doubt red in the face, I wasn't in the mood for visitors.

"Oh, my dear, you do have a job on your hands, don't you?" The elderly woman with bronzed skin, deep wrinkles, and stark white hair smiled, red lipstick smeared across her teeth. I automatically rubbed my fingers across my teeth.

"What's that?" she asked. "Oh!" After dealing with the lipstick mishap, she opened the screen door and heaved a cooler bag toward me. "I brought you this. A welcoming gift."

"Thank you. That wasn't necessary." I took the bag from her, staggering under the weight.

"Nonsense. You're new to town. It's the neighborly thing to do."

"Oh, so you live next door?" I jerked my thumb toward the house next to mine.

"What? Oh, no. I live on the Esplanade. Oh my goodness, silly me, I forgot to introduce myself. I'm Doris Shutt." She held out her hand.

Placing the cooler at my feet, I shook her hand, pondering her name. Doris Shutt. As in… the door is shut?

"Hi, Doris. I'm Holly." I couldn't bring myself to tell her my surname. The humiliation was still raw.

"Pleased to meet you, Holly. I hear you're a relative of John's? We didn't think he had any family. He never spoke of them."

"He was my mother's uncle—they were estranged. It took the lawyers a while to track me down." The lie rolled off my tongue with ease, and Doris nodded in understanding.

"Ahhh, I see. Well, John did tend to keep to himself, so that doesn't surprise me. Mind if I come in?" A bit late for that, considering she was already standing in my living room. She tsk'd, hands-on-hips as she surveyed the state of things. "This is quite the job."

I couldn't contain the sigh that fell out of my mouth. "I admit it wasn't quite what I was expecting. The lawyers said Uncle John had property. I'm not sure this qualifies."

"Hmmm," she sucked in her cheeks and released them with a pop. "We're going to need help."

"We?" It wasn't until I moved that Doris noticed my foot, the folds of my skirt having hidden the walking boot from view.

"Holy cockadoodles, girl, what have you done to yourself? Here, sit, sit." She tried to guide me toward the armchair, but there was no way I was sitting on that thing. For an old lady she had the driving force of a Mack truck, and I had to plant my feet to stop her from tipping me into the chair.

"It's fine. Just a small break that will heal quickly," I protested. "And FYI, I'm not sitting on that." I pointed to the stained chair, nose wrinkling in disgust. I'd rather sit on the floor. Doris stopped pushing me and eyed the armchair.

"You could be right." She harrumphed. "That does look like it needs—"

"Burning?"

She tipped back her head and laughed, a loud, joyful sound. "Exactly. This whole place needs razing to the ground and starting over."

"Yeah, but then I'd have nowhere to live."

Her eyes narrowed, her expression shrewd. "You're intending to stay?"

I shrugged. "For a while." Until the SIA found their mole and shut down the counterfeit wand operation. Then I'd be leaving Gravestone and getting on with my life. But Doris didn't need to know that.

"Right. Well. This won't do. We need supplies." She hustled to the door. I'd hoped to air the place out, but the heat from outside, mingling with the heat from inside, made the entire house an overheated, stinking cesspool.

"You find somewhere to sit down and help yourself to refreshments from the cooler," Doris instructed. "I'll be back in a jiffy."

CHAPTER
Three

Not twenty minutes later, Doris returned. When she'd said reinforcements, she'd meant it. At least ten women trailed in behind her, complete with aprons and rubber gloves, carrying buckets, mops, sponges, and rags. All of them sported varying shades of red lipstick. It was a good thing I was sitting down on the makeshift seat I'd made of an overturned bucket because the sight of these women was enough to strike fear into the heart of the bravest of men.

Flynn sat on my shoulder, begging for crumbs from the energy bar I was eating, unfazed by the gray army. I glanced at him out of the corner of my eye. Was he preening? I snorted. Figured. Flynn had always been a ladies' man. Present him with a roomful of beauties, and of course, he was going to puff out his chest and try to impress. Sadly, it seemed he'd forgotten that, currently, he was a rat.

"Holly, I'd like you to meet Bernadette Bridge, Vera Cherrington, Carmella Highwater, Ethel Dawes, Gladys Overwith, Valda Collins, Ophelia Paine, Denise Hurt, and the two Ada's. Ada Rose Bartlett and Ada Florence Holmes. Ladies, meet Holly."

Doris rattled through the names so quickly they were a blur, but a few of them caught my attention. Denise Hurt? As in, the knees hurt? And Carmella Highwater. Come hell or high water. My brow furrowed. What was it with this town and people's names? Was it a thing? A requirement of living here?

One of the Adas bobbed in a curtsy, making me smile. "What was your last name, dear? Is it Smith, like your uncle?"

"Great uncle, and no. My last name is Day."

Doris clapped. "Holly Day! Adorable."

"I'm glad you think so," I grumbled beneath my breath. No one heard because the average age of my group of helpers had to be seventy at the very least. I suspected they'd all been dying to get a stickybeak inside of John Smith's home as they nudged each other and contemplated the job at hand.

"Ladies, ladies," Doris shouted over the din of ten elderly women all talking at once and exclaiming what an utter dump the place was and how they'd had no idea. "Divide and conquer. This is to be Holly's home, and we can't have her living in these conditions. It's up to us to do our neighborly duty and show Holly that she is welcome here."

"Welcome, Holly," one of the women, I couldn't recall her name, maybe Denise, said. She held up the cleaning basket she was holding. "I clean the mayor's offices, and the library, a little dust and dirt is no problem." We were dealing with a little more than dust and dirt, but I kept my thoughts to myself. No need to kill their enthusiasm.

"What about the furniture?" one of the Adas asked, pointing to the disgusting sofa and armchair. Doris tapped her lip as if considering that we could actually save them somehow. All the bleach in the world would not convince me to sit on either of them.

"I say we drag them outside and burn them," I said from my position on the overturned bucket. "Nice night for a bonfire, right?"

Ada beamed in delight. "Yay!" She clapped. "We haven't had a fire in ages. How exciting."

"What will Holly sit on, though? If we burn her furniture?" the other Ada chimed in.

"Not to worry, I have it covered. The deputy is dropping by with some camping equipment for us to borrow," Doris said.

"You recruited the deputy to help as well? In what?" I glanced at my watch. "Under half an hour?"

"You'll come to learn that I'm a very resourceful woman, Holly Day."

"Please." I grimaced. "Just Holly." I'd prefer Twitch, but that was off-limits until this whole sorry mess was sorted.

While the women got busy dragging out items for the bonfire, scrubbing floors and walls, and boxing up John's personal things for me to go through later, I planted myself at the kitchen sink and began the tedious task of scrubbing what remained of my great uncle's cutlery and crockery, such as it was. Nothing matched, half of it was broken, and the remaining half had to be decades old. Flynn figured the best vantage point was my shoulder, and since I'd feel bad if he got stepped on, I allowed it. I was getting used to having him around but quickly learned to establish a few boundaries. No following me into the bathroom, and steer clear of the boobage.

"Knock, knock," a woman's voice called from the front of the house.

"Come on through," I called back. "I'm in the kitchen."

Up to my elbows in suds, I looked up to see the deputy walk in, hand resting loosely on the holster at her hip.

"Hi," I said, eyeing her up and down. I hadn't expected the deputy to be a woman for some reason. Sexist, I know, but in a town this size, I'd just assumed the law enforcement contingent would all be male. But this deputy was very much of the female persuasion, ample curves threatening to pop the buttons of her shirt, blonde hair pulled back into a ponytail beneath her hat. I put her to be in her late twenties at the very least.

"You must be Holly." She nodded in greeting. "I'm deputy Laura Biden. Just call me Laura. I've got a few things to help you out while you get settled. They're just in the back of my truck. Where do you want them?"

"What are they?"

"A fold-up camping chair, a cot, bedding."

"The living room will be fine. I'll set up camp in there for now until I get the rest of the house sorted." We'd basically stripped the living room of all furniture except for the television and a massive bookcase that was sturdy and worth saving. I'd go through the books crammed onto the shelves later. The filthy old rug covering the floor had been rolled up and dragged outside, leaving the floorboards bare.

"Heck of a job."

"Actually, you might be able to tell me something. Did John die here? In the house? Specifically in the armchair or bed?"

What I can only describe as surprise passed across her face before she schooled her features. "You don't know?"

I frowned. "Where he died? No. I don't. We were estranged. I wasn't aware I had a great uncle at all until the lawyers found me."

"And they didn't tell you how he died?" she pressed.

I froze. Flynn clutched a strand of hair for balance, stood on his hind legs, and sniffed the air, whiskers twitching. "How he died?"

"I'm surprised none of the welcoming committee told you." Laura shook her head, running a hand around the nape of her neck as if annoyed that she was the one who had to deliver the news. Whatever the news was, I suspected it wasn't good.

"Just tell me," I prompted, removing my hands from the sink and tugging off the yellow rubber gloves.

"John Smith killed himself."

Wow. Had not been expecting that. "How?"

"Hung himself."

I automatically glanced up at the ceiling.

"Not here. Out back." Laura pointed out the grimy window above the sink.

"In the shed?" The back yard was in worse shape than the front, weeds shoulder height. However, the committee of women who'd come to help had beaten down a path and was dumping rubbish and ruined furniture in a pile away from the house, ready for the bonfire. To the right was a shed, big enough to house a car. Which reminded me I should check if John had a set of wheels I could use.

"No. The tree."

The cedar elm in question was massive, towering over the shed, its branches reaching the house. Any of its branches would easily have held the weight of a swinging body. Although it was quite the feat for a seventy-year-old to heave himself up into the tree with a rope around his neck.

"Are you okay?" Laura asked, taking a step closer,

clearly worried I was upset about the demise of my great uncle.

"I'm fine," I assured her. "I mean, yeah, it's sad and all, but I didn't know him. At all. I didn't know a single thing about him."

"Your mom didn't tell you anything?"

"My mom died when I was eighteen," I lied smoothly. "And up until that point, she hadn't mentioned once that she had family. As far as I knew, she was an only child, orphaned at five, and grew up in foster homes." The lie wasn't too far from the truth. My mom did die. Only I'd been eight, and I was the one who grew up in foster homes.

"Regardless. I'm sorry for your loss." But her eyes weren't on me. They were on Flynn. "I'm not sure if you're aware," she said, hand slowly reaching for her gun, "but you have a rodent on your shoulder."

"Don't shoot!" I urged, holding out a hand to stop her. "He's my pet. He's harmless." Flynn tensed at my words, annoyed that I'd described him as my pet and doubly outraged that he was a non-threat. In human form, he was formidable. Had to be when you were an SIA agent. As a wolf shifter, he was practically indestructible. But now, when he was the size of his own hand? Not so much.

Laura remained frozen, eyes on the rat who stood taller and eyeballed her, refusing to back down. "Flynn. Quit it," I whispered out the corner of my mouth. He shot me a look, shook his head, then turned his attention back to the deputy.

Slowly, she released her grip on her gun, which fell back into its holster with an audible thunk. "Sorry," she muttered, straightening her shoulders. "I've never met anyone who keeps a rodent as a pet. Usually, we exterminate them. I'll just go get those things for you and be on my way."

She hightailed it out of the kitchen before I could say another word, but I caught the red in her cheeks as she passed through the doorway and knew she was uncomfortable about Flynn's presence. Minutes later, I heard the clatter as she dumped the camping gear in the living room, then called out a farewell.

"Bye. Thanks!" I belatedly replied, doubting she heard me over the rumble of her truck as it pulled away.

"She couldn't get out of here quick enough," I said to Flynn, who nodded his head in agreement, then shot down my back and jumped, launching himself off my butt to land with the grace of a gymnast on the floor. He shot me a look over his shoulder before scurrying out of the kitchen and into the living room, no doubt to check out what the deputy had delivered.

"If I find you napping in there," I called out, "there will be hell to pay."

"Who are you talking to?" Doris stepped inside, her cheeks flushed from the heat. I chewed my lip, it having only just dawned on me that I had nearly a dozen senior citizens doing manual labor in the heat of the day. These conditions couldn't be good for any of them.

"My pet rat. Flynn," I answered absently, glancing

out the window above the sink. I could just make out a few figures tossing items on the bonfire pile through the filthy pane. The rest of the women had to be inside, either in the living room or upstairs. I'd been so lost in my own thoughts while scrubbing the dirty dishes that I'd failed to keep track of them. Not even a full day in Gravestone, and I was losing my touch.

"You have a rat? Cool! Where is he?" Doris began scouring the floor to see if she could spot him.

"He's in the living room, probably checking out the gear the deputy just dropped off. He's gray and white, wearing a harness." I probably should have told the women earlier about Flynn's presence. Still, they hadn't noticed him when they'd first arrived, despite him sitting on my shoulder, and I hadn't thought of it afterward. "Is everyone okay?" I chewed my lip and glanced outside again. "It's sweltering today."

Doris waved a hand in dismissal. "Oh, they're fine. We're used to it."

I wasn't convinced. "Maybe we should take a break?" The last thing I needed was one of them keeling over. Harding had told me, multiple times, to keep a low profile. Having a senior citizen pass out from heatstroke would not be what he considered a low profile.

"I'll hand out some drinks," Doris said, heading to the cooler she'd brought with her earlier. I watched her pull out a bottle of water and a stack of dixie cups. Had they been in the cooler all along? I hadn't noticed them when I'd helped myself to a drink while waiting for Doris and her crew.

"Maybe we should work on the fridge next," Doris suggested. "This cooler won't hold you for long."

"Actually, that's something I noticed," I said, hobbling across to the mustard-colored fridge. "The power is on. Was it never disconnected? Or did someone know I was coming and had it reconnected?" In which case, I must thank them.

Doris shrugged. "Can't help you there, I'm afraid. But maybe be careful when you open that door, hmmm? If the power has been off for any length of time, then whatever is in that fridge is probably a gloopy mess."

I stopped my forward momentum and took a step back. "Hadn't thought of that."

Before I could stop her, Doris zipped across the floor —she was remarkably agile for a woman of her vintage —and flung open the door. The light inside illuminated an almost empty fridge. No decomposing sludge to be seen. She turned and beamed at me in delight. "There you go! All good. I'll just give it a quick wipe-down. We'll toss that old milk carton and whatever is hiding in the back."

"I can do that," I offered, feeling guilty that not only had I hesitated over the prospect of a stinky fridge, but I'd let an old woman handle it. "You've done so much for me already."

"Nonsense." She slammed the fridge door shut with such force the whole thing shuddered. "You need to go sit down. You should be resting that foot, not walking around on it."

I allowed her to usher me into the living room, where she deftly unfolded the camping chair and guided me into it. Guided was probably too polite. Shoved me into it was more apt. I got the sense that it was useless arguing with Doris Shutt once she'd turned her mind to something.

CHAPTER
Four

"**H**old it!"

Everyone froze. We were standing around the pile of junk in the back yard, admiring the towering combination of broken and stained furniture, clothing that could walk on its own, and trash. It really was a work of art, equally enthralling as it was appalling. The sun was beating a hasty retreat over the horizon, painting the sky in a riot of purples, pinks, and oranges so stunning it took my breath away. It had been too long since I'd stood and just enjoyed the beauty of a sunset. It was especially majestic viewed through a mountain of trash.

"Ada Rose, you blow that match out immediately." Sheriff Joshua Calder strode around the corner of the house, hands-on-hips, expression stern. "The deputy warned me you lot were up to something. Seems I arrived just in time."

"What's up?" I whispered to Doris out of the corner

of my mouth, for the sheriff seemed riled, and we hadn't done anything wrong. Had we? Ada quickly blew out the match before it burned her fingers.

"Pft, it's nothing," she whispered back. "Sheriff has got his panties in a wad over nothing."

"I heard that, Doris." His head snapped around, and he pinned the old lady by my side with a look that should have had her quaking with fear. I expected a tongue lashing to ensue, but he merely sighed and shook his head. "How many times, ladies?"

There was a shuffling of feet and non-committal murmuring, but no one answered him. I nudged Doris. "How many times for what?"

Before she could answer, the sheriff continued. "No fires." He pointed to the impressive mountain of furniture, boxes, and rubbish we'd accumulated. "That needs to go to the dump."

"Why no fires?" I asked. He turned to me. "I'll give you the benefit of the doubt since you're new here, and you probably come from the city where such things aren't on your radar, but out here? It's fire danger season. And you light up a pile of trash with all this dry grass and undergrowth around? Well, you may as well light up a match for the entire town of Gravestone."

I examined the tall, brown grass and weeds. He was right on both counts. There was a lot of undergrowth here that would make an excellent fuel source for a fire, and it hadn't crossed my mind that the fire could potentially get out of control. Usually, I'd use my magic for such things, but it wasn't an option since my magic was on lockdown.

"You're absolutely right," I told him. "I apologize."

He blinked, taken aback, then gave a curt nod. "Accepted. Like I said, you weren't to know differently. But this lot?" He pointed to each and every woman standing around the intended fire. "You do know better. No fires in summer. It's too dangerous."

"You should have told me," I hissed to Doris, annoyed that I was in the wrong. I didn't like being in the wrong. It felt like I was at a disadvantage, and that rankled worse than wearing underwear two sizes too small. Don't ask me how I know that.

"It would have been fine," she hissed back.

"Can't believe I have a bunch of pyromaniacs on my hands," the sheriff mumbled to himself, snatching the box of matches out of Ada Rose's hands.

"Apologies once again, Sheriff," I soothed. "Now that I know, I'll make sure no one lights this baby up. But... I'm without a vehicle. Any suggestions on how I can get this trash removed?"

"I'll speak with Ken for you," he said, softening slightly. "Ken Opener has a truck, and for a few dollars, he'll take this lot off your hands."

My mouth dropped open. "Ken Opener? Are you serious?"

"What?"

Before I could point out the obvious, Flynn came scurrying across the yard. His squeaks and chatter drew our attention, and I looked on with mild amusement as he dragged… I wasn't sure what it was, but it was bigger than him, making it awkward as he struggled to make his way to my feet, where he dropped the object and looked up at me expectantly, waiting.

The sheriff took a hasty step away from the rat, and I smirked at his fear of a creature a fraction of his size. Then I had a closer look at what Flynn had brought me. Reaching down, I picked it up, the late afternoon sun bouncing off the white bones of a hand and forearm.

"Is that…" Doris reached into the pocket of her apron for her glasses and slid them on, taking a closer look. "Well, I'll be damned."

"Yep." I nodded. "It's a hand. A human hand."

"But it's a prop, right?" Valda asked, hand to her throat, twisting the pearls she wore.

"Must be an old Halloween decoration," Ada Rose said.

"Why would Flynn sniff it out then?" Doris pointed out. "The rat isn't going to be attracted to plastic."

As if to prove her point, the wrist detached from the ulna. It plummeted to the ground, leaving me holding the radius with the rest of the hand precariously attached. A gasp echoed around the abandoned bonfire.

The sheriff stepped forward, ignoring Flynn, who'd shot up my leg when the bone had dropped. "I'll take that. Doris, grab me one of your garbage bags. An unused one," he added.

"On it." She hurried away, returning seconds later, shaking out a garbage bag and holding it open. The sheriff took the bones from me and carefully placed them in the bag, then picked up the ulna lying at my feet. "Human remains," he said under his breath.

And that's when Ada Florence threw up. All over me.

"Urgh!" I cried, jumping back, only my fractured foot prevented such sudden movements, and pain shot up my leg, and I crumpled to the ground. Flynn leaped clear, and rather than sticking around to make sure I was okay, he hightailed it back inside the house, squeezing through the rat-sized hole in the screen door.

I lay there for a moment, winded, covered in dirt and vomit, and wondered how my life had become this. Then Doris's face came into view. "You okay there, Holly? Sorry about Ada Florence. She has a weak stomach."

"So I see," I grumbled, maneuvering to my hands and knees. My foot was throbbing. I'd already done too much today, and that sudden jerk had been the last straw. My poor navicular was never going to heal at this rate. I had a high pain threshold. Probably too high. And my fractured foot had just let me know in no uncertain terms that enough was enough.

Doris helped me to my feet, and it pained me to have to rely on someone else's assistance as I hobbled toward the house.

"Hey!" the sheriff called out. "You can't leave. We aren't done here."

I halted but didn't turn around. "I'm going to get changed. I'm covered in vomit, and seriously, I don't know what Ada Florence has been eating—possibly prunes—but I'm going to hurl myself if I have to keep breathing it in."

There was a moment's silence then, "Very well. Be quick about it. I need to question you."

This time, I turned my head, one brow raised. "Really? So, you think it's feasible that I could be responsible for this?" I jerked my head toward the garbage bag he was carrying. "Despite only arriving in town today, I somehow managed to murder some poor soul and hide their body on my great uncle's property. I mean, I'm good, but I didn't know I was that good."

Doris snorted next to me, then helped me up the back step and inside. "I'll be fine from here," I told her, leaning against the kitchen counter while I rummaged through my bag for my bottle of pain pills. "Let the sheriff know I'll be out in due course. I'm going to take a quick shower. Ada's upchuck is stinging my skin something awful." It wasn't a lie. It was like her stomach acids were burning through my skin, not to mention the stench. My stomach rolled in protest.

I tossed back a couple of pills, heard the screen door slam, then, making sure no one was watching, I crawled up the stairs. Crawled! The only bathroom in the house was upstairs, sandwiched between the two bedrooms, and despite having decided to camp out downstairs while I got the house in order, I hadn't anticipated the bathroom situation.

Once I reached the landing, I hauled myself to my feet and limped into the bathroom, annoyed to discover the door wouldn't close behind me. It was so warped it had no hope of fitting within the frame, no matter how much I put my shoulder to it. In the end, I left it, deciding no one was going to disturb me anyway, so what did it matter?

Thankfully, the bathroom had been cleaned, and over the smell of vomit permeating my nostrils, I could detect the faint scent of bleach. Turning on the taps in the shower, I unstrapped the walking boot, stripped off my clothes, and tossed them against the door in some wild semblance of keeping it shut while the water heated, then stepped beneath the spray. Of course, I hadn't brought in my toiletries, so it was just me and the water, but it was better than nothing. I scrubbed off Ava's vomit and the day's grime, then turned off the water before realizing besides toiletries, I also didn't have a towel.

"Unbelievable." Staring at the ceiling, I let myself drip dry for a moment while I contemplated what color I should paint the ceiling. White was the logical choice, but maybe I'd go crazy and choose something outrageous like yellow. Or blue. I'd never decorated a house before, but it was abundantly clear that John Smith's house was in desperate need of renovation. Of course, I'd come into the bathroom without bringing in a clean set of clothes, which annoyed me even more because usually, I was on top of everything. But today hadn't been a typical day, and I was definitely off my game.

Snatching up my walking boot, I examined it, relieved that none of Ada's vomit had reached it. It was dusty and dirty, but I'd give it a wipe down before retiring for the night. Clutching it to my chest, I hopped out of the bathroom and into the bedroom where I'd left my suitcase. Rummaging through the contents, I settled on a pair of denim shorts and a T-shirt. Tugging my underwear and clothing on over damp skin was a herculean effort that made me sweat. By the time I was dressed, I needed another shower already. Pulling my hair into a wet ponytail, I strapped my foot back into the walking boot and eased myself down the stairs on my butt.

"Here she is," Doris said when I appeared in the kitchen. "I told you she wouldn't be long."

"Where is everyone?" The kitchen was fast becoming my favorite room. The army of white-haired little old ladies had done a fantastic job, passing through the house in a cleaning frenzy, and now that I could see the bones of the house, I'd decided it wasn't so bad. Although I was hoping I wouldn't be here long enough for it to matter. But having a project to keep me occupied would help pass the time. And keep me out of trouble.

The kitchen cabinets were solid timber, worn, but a coat of paint or stain would bring them back to life. The kitchen table had been salvaged. Once the trash had been removed, a quick wipe down, and she was as good as new. Sort of. A few dings and scratches added character. The fridge had scrubbed up okay as well, but the oven? There was no saving it. I made a mental note to ask Ken Opener if he'd be able to remove it for me. And where I'd likely find a replacement.

"Sent them home," the sheriff said, stepping inside. He was no longer carrying the plastic bag with the bones. "Take a seat."

I didn't like his tone. It was the tone you used when you thought someone was guilty of something. But how could I possibly be a suspect when I'd only been in Gravestone five minutes?

"Did you find the rest of the body?" I asked, sliding onto one of the two chairs. Doris took the remaining seat, leaving the sheriff standing. Which gave him the upper hand, towering over us.

He looked surprised that I'd asked but quickly covered it, a shutter coming down so I couldn't read his expression. "I did not. But we'll be back tomorrow to conduct a thorough search."

"Any idea who the victim is?"

"Bit hard to tell from a skeletal hand," he drawled, crossing his arms across his chest.

"Yes, but this is a small town. If anyone were to go missing, I'm sure you'd know about it. Taking into consideration the weather, and the condition of the bones, I'd say that body has been in the ground for at least three to six months. Anyone go missing around then?"

His brow furrowed, and his eyes narrowed. "How on earth would you know that?"

Think fast. "I work in a bookstore." I shrugged nonchalantly. "When it's not busy, I read books."

Doris winked at me, and it was my turn to look taken aback. Did she know? But she couldn't. There was no way she could possibly know the truth. No way.

The sun had finished setting while I was in the shower, and now, darkness crept in. Along with it, noises. Night-time noises. There was something else as well. The silence. If you tuned out the hum of insects and croaking of frogs from the mangrove, it was eerily silent. I was used to the hum of traffic, voices, the sounds of daily living. Out here, there was nothing but quiet. I wasn't sure I liked it.

I stood and hobbled to the back door, closing it. Doris and the sheriff watched. "What?" I said defensively. "Didn't either of you see that enormous hole in the fly screen? I don't want the mosquitos getting in."

Doris rummaged in her bag and pulled out a bottle, slamming it down on the table. "I'll leave you some insect repellant," she said, then stood. "Sheriff, I think it's time you and I left Holly to get some rest. She's looking a little peaky, wouldn't you agree?"

The sheriff studied me. "She looks tired, yes."

I snorted. Any wonder I was tired? It had been one heck of a day, but still, I bristled that they'd felt the need to point out how awful I looked.

The sheriff indicated Doris should precede him through the kitchen door into the living room. "I'll be back in the morning," he said to me.

"Fine."

"Call me if you need anything," Doris called with a wave. "I already put my number in your phone."

My eyebrows shot up into my hairline. Hurrying as fast as my busted foot would allow, I reached my bag that was still sitting on the kitchen counter and rummaged around until I found the burner phone Harding had given me. Navigating to the contacts, I saw I had a new number stored. The only number stored. Doris Shutt. The front door slammed, and I called out a belated farewell. Seconds later, a text arrived from Doris.

"The bones belong to Seth Saltzman. He was murdered."

Doris's text made sleep impossible. Not to mention the heat. I'd had to close the doors and windows to keep the mosquitos out, and despite the sun having set hours ago, the house retained the heat. I lay on the cot in a tank top and panties, the walking boot on the floor, and tried not to think about my discomfort. I listened to the sounds of the house settling and the unfamiliar noises coming from the mangroves. Doris had told me alligators weren't so common anymore, which was comforting, I guess.

Exhaustion pulled at me, but sleep was elusive. Apparently, Flynn didn't have the same problem. He was splayed on his back on the camp chair, spread-eagled and sound asleep. Some bodyguard he was.

"This is impossible," I huffed, giving up on the idea that I'd get any sleep tonight. Sitting up, I swung my feet over the side of the cot, strapped on the walking boot, and limped to the kitchen. I'd retrieved my laptop from my suitcase earlier, and now, I opened it and connected to the internet via a hotspot on my cell phone. Foot propped up on the other chair, I googled Seth Saltzman. There were a few of them. The top results were for a professional musician, but he was very much alive, so clearly, he wasn't our victim. Sweeping my hair up into a messy bun, I fanned my face and pondered Doris's text. How had she known?

Picking up my phone, I sent Doris a text. "Did you kill him?"

I wasn't expecting an immediate answer considering it was three in the morning, so when my phone dinged, I jumped.

"Would it matter if I did?" Doris wrote.

"No. But it would help to know if I need to help you hide the rest of the body." It was a joke. Sort of.

"I knew there was a reason I liked you." Before I could reply, another message arrived. "Get some sleep. We'll talk in the morning."

Putting the phone aside, I pulled a notepad out of my bag and began scribbling out a list of items I'd need for the house. Besides a new oven, I'd need sheets and towels and a flashlight. I looked longingly out the kitchen window—what I could see through the filth anyway—eager to go looking for the rest of Seth Saltzman's remains, but there was no way I could do so without a flashlight. There was barely any moon tonight, visibility was beyond poor, and I didn't know the lay of the land. Knowing how my luck was going, I'd probably misstep and end up in the mangroves.

I reached for the thermos of coffee Doris had brought with her, but it was long since empty. Sighing, I added a coffee maker to my list. If I was going to pull an all-nighter, I would need caffeine. I rested my elbow on the table and propped my head on my hand while I pondered my list. Paint. Lots of it. But I'd need to work out whether I needed to replace any drywall before painting, and that was beyond my area of expertise. I made a note to ask Doris if she knew any builders or contractors in the area. Lucky for me, I had an expense account that was disguised as my inheritance. My fake great uncle certainly hadn't been spending money on keeping his house in order. Therefore, it shouldn't surprise anyone that he had a healthy bank balance. I had no idea if that were true or not, but as far as cover stories went, it worked.

While I was mentally walking through the house, noting the obvious things that needed fixing—like the bathroom door—I must have drifted off, for the next thing I knew, someone was banging on the front door, and sunlight was streaming through the kitchen window.

"Okay, okay, I'm coming!" I yelled when the banging showed no signs of easing. It wasn't a standard knock. It was one of those fists-to-the-wood-you'd-better-open-up-or-else type knocks. I'd expected the owner of that demanding summons to be the sheriff, but color me surprised when it was Doris on the other side of the door.

"Oh good, you're up." She beamed. Today, she was wearing camouflage cargo pants, a yellow and pink floral blouse tucked into the pants, a thin silver belt threaded through the belt loops, and bright fuchsia lipstick. On her feet was a sturdy pair of black hiking boots.

I blinked. "Did you bring coffee?"

"Of course." She pushed past me, brandishing a thermos. "Go get dressed while I pour us a cup, and be quick about it. We need to search for Seth's body before Calder gets here."

"Calder?" I was losing track of names.

"The sheriff. FYI, no one calls him Sheriff. We all call him Calder, so...."

"So, if I want to fit in, stop calling him Sheriff is what you're saying." Good to know. I headed upstairs as fast as I could manage, used the bathroom, and pulled on denim shorts and a clean tank top before heading back downstairs to find Doris waiting at the foot of the stairs with the requisite cup of coffee.

"Thanks." Without missing a beat, I took a sip and headed for the back door. "Lock the front door, will you?" I said to Doris over my shoulder.

"Why? There's nothing worth stealing."

"No, but I don't want the sher—Calder—walking in unannounced."

She chuckled. "I like it. You're not going to make it

easy for him." I heard her turn the bolt on the door, then her hurried footsteps as she caught up with me.

"You didn't answer my question last night," I said conversationally, stepping onto the back deck, then down the steps.

"The answer is no. I didn't kill him."

I'd figured as much, but I was quickly learning not to take the citizens of Gravestone for granted.

"How do you know it's Seth Saltzman?"

"Because he went missing three months ago. Everyone figured he'd left town."

"No doubt Calder has come to the same conclusion." I stopped to take another swig of coffee. As the caffeine started to circulate through my system, my synapses began to fire, and a surge of energy shot through me. This, I could do. Hunt a killer. The thrill of the chase sent a spike of adrenaline surging through me, and I turned to Doris. "Who do you know who would want Seth Saltzman dead?"

"Oh, pretty much everyone in town," she replied. She pointed toward the shed. "I think Flynn came from that direction."

I headed that way. "Why did everyone hate him? What did he do?"

Doris harrumphed. "He lied about having cancer! We all rallied around him, held fundraisers to help him pay for treatment. And every week, he'd head to Corpus Christi for his *chemo* and gamble away the money we'd given him."

"Wow. No wonder he wasn't liked." Reason enough to kill him? Possibly. Especially if you'd contributed a lot of money to his fundraiser. Money was definitely a motive for wanting someone dead. "You said he disappeared?"

The shed had double doors at one end and a single side door for easy access. I tried the side door first. Locked. And I'd only had one key on my keyring, and that unlocked the front door to the house. Another mental note. Hire a locksmith.

"Yeah, a few days after he got found out. We figured he'd packed a bag and hightailed it out of here."

Doris followed me to the front of the shed, where I pulled on the doors. Surprisingly, they opened with little effort but a lot of screeching. Doris took one door, I took the other, and we pulled them back, wedging them open with a strategically placed rock on either side.

We stood at the open shed, taking in the contents. I'd been expecting it to be as bad, if not worse than, the house. But it actually wasn't in too bad a shape. In the center of the garage was a beat-up pickup. The faded red and silver 1988 Chevrolet had seen better days, and I wondered if it still ran. Probably needed a new battery. And new tires. A metal frame was rigged in the back.

"How did Seth get found out?" I asked, making my way between the pickup and the shelves that lined the shed toward the small storage area at the far end.

"A girl, how else?" Doris sniffed, following me on the opposite side of the pickup. "Seems he'd been having a dalliance with a Corpus Christi lass, and she must've got a wee bit impatient for his weekly visits, so she decided to pay him a visit in Gravestone. Two problems. For one, he was already dating a girl here. And as soon as the locals figured she knew Seth, they started offering her their condolences and asking how she was holding up and all that type of thing. And that's when she dropped him in it, telling everyone he wasn't sick and that each week he came down to Corpus Christi, he'd invite her to the fancy hotel he was staying at, and they'd live it up. She mistakenly thought he was rich."

"They confronted him?"

Doris nodded. "Demanded to see doctors' reports and scans and all. Of course, he had none of that because he was fleecing us all." Doris cleared her throat. "Then the law got involved 'cos things got a wee bit… heated."

"Seth was charged?"

Doris nodded. "Court case pending."

"But then he disappeared, and everyone thought he'd done a runner."

"It fits."

At the back of the shed was a large workbench. Sitting on the bench was a cardboard box with the words *scrap for John* written on the side. I lifted a flap and peeked inside. It was full of offcuts of timber. On the wall above the workbench hung multiple tools. The setup was the opposite of the chaos and neglect inside the house.

"Was John Smith a carpenter?" I asked Doris, eyeing

the saws, hammers, and jars containing nails, nuts, and bolts.

"Why yes, he was. Why do you ask?"

"No reason." Other than the man had the tools and obviously the skills to maintain his home, yet he didn't.

"That old bookcase in the house? John made that. And the kitchen table," Doris said.

"Yet, he let his home fall into a state of disrepair."

"Pft, that's not so unusual. Just like painters have the worst painted house on the street. John was a grumpy old man, but he sure knew his way around a piece of wood. I doubt there's a home in Gravestone that doesn't have a piece of his work."

I ran my finger along the workbench, then studied my filthy finger and the clean mark I'd left behind. No one had been in the shed for a long time.

"Well, I'm not seeing skeletal remains in here," I said, dusting my hands together.

"Under the pickup, maybe?" Doris suggested.

"Really? You think if you'd killed a man, you'd hide his body beneath a pickup?"

She had the grace to look sheepish. "Worth a try. Maybe John didn't kill him? Maybe Seth was here to steal stuff and died of natural causes."

"Under John's truck." I did not believe for one second that Seth Saltzman's body was underneath the pickup, but to humor her, I got to my hands and knees and peered underneath. Besides a long since dried oil stain, nothing was beneath the truck. Using the hood, I pulled myself back to my feet. "Flynn must've found the bones outside," I said, making my way back to the double doors.

When Calder arrived, we were behind the shed, poking around in the weeds.

"Figured I'd find you sticking your nose in where it doesn't belong," he said from behind us, making us both jump. That was the second time he'd walked up on me without me noticing.

"I'd hardly call it poking my nose in, considering this is my property." I turned to face him, ready to argue, but the disarming grin on his face took the wind clean out of my sales.

"What she said," Doris said. "Bout time you got here, Calder. What time do you call this?" She tapped her watch as if we'd been waiting for him to show for hours.

"I call it eight o'clock, Doris. And even that is too early to be calling on folks," Calder shot back, then his eyes turned to me. "What time did she turn up?"

I shrugged, not prepared to throw my new friend under the bus. "Oh, a few minutes ago. I was already out here." I was used to lying. It was in my job description, after all. I fooled most folks, but I suspected Calder wasn't fooled, not one hundred percent anyway. But he let it go.

"You find the rest of the bones?" he asked. "I see you've already searched the garage."

"No skeleton in there," I agreed. "But good to know John had a set of wheels."

"You make sure it's legal before you take it on the

road. Can you even drive with that thing on?" He eyed my walking boot.

"If it's an automatic, it shouldn't be a problem." Despite the doctor saying no driving, I had no intentions of being stuck at the house on my own until I healed.

Calder's eyes drifted from my walking boot up my body, coming to rest somewhere around my chest area.

"Enjoying the perv?" I snapped, crossing my arms over my chest in irritation.

"What? No!" He blushed beet red and held his hands up in a stop gesture. "No, sorry, I wasn't looking at your," he waved his hands around, "your, you know…."

"My breasts?"

"Exactly. No." He cleared his throat, though his bright red color remained. "I was looking at that mark on your collarbone. Is that a burn?"

My hand went to the mark in question. "No. It's a birthmark."

"Lemme see." Doris grabbed my shoulder and spun me to face her. She put on her glasses and stood with her face inches from my chest while she peered at the mark in question. "Interesting." She took her glasses off and slid them back into the pocket of her pants.

"What is?" I knew it was trouble asking, but I couldn't help myself. I didn't know why they were both getting so excited over a stupid birthmark. Usually, it was hidden beneath my clothing, but with the spaghetti straps of my tank, it was on clear display.

"That, my dear, is a rune. Algiz, to be precise. It means defense and protection, a shield to guard against evil."

As soon as the words left Doris's mouth, Flynn chose that moment to bite Doris's ankle. Hard. She shrieked in surprise and pain. Calder drew his gun and took a shot at Flynn, who scampered into the weeds for cover. My reaction was automatic and instinctive. I lunged at Calder and punched him in the jaw.

Six

I guess if you wanted to get a little peace and quiet, a cell in Gravestone PD was the place to do it. At the back of the station, which suspiciously looked like an ordinary house if it weren't for the police sign out front, were two cells, each containing two cots and a toilet hidden behind a half wall for some semblance of privacy.

Currently, I was the only resident.

Lying back on the cot, I laced my fingers beneath my head and stared up at the ceiling, watching the blades of the metal fan as it lazily spun around and around over my head. "I'm going to need fans," I said to myself, going through my mental list for things that needed fixing at the house. "Or even better, AC."

"I can lend you a pedestal fan," Doris said from the bars separating my cell from the passageway. I didn't bother looking up. I'd heard her yelling at Calder from back here and knew it was only a matter of time before she turned up to visit me.

"That'd be great, Doris. Thanks."

"I'm sorry about what happened."

That got my attention. I sat up and eyeballed the crazy old bat. "Something tells me people don't often get an apology out of you." I watched through narrowed eyes, searching for traces that what she was going to say next was a lie.

"If Calder hadn't been so trigger-happy, none of this would have happened," she deflected.

I flopped backward, resuming my study of the fan. "Damn straight. But while we're apologizing, I'm sorry my rat bit you." That was the only thing in this whole sorry mess that bothered me. Why did Flynn bite her? It was so out of character.

"He bit me because I stepped on his tail," Doris said. "Pretty natural reaction if you ask me."

"You did?" I hadn't even known Flynn had followed us out to the shed, let alone that Doris had accidentally stepped on him.

Doris wrung her hands. "I hope he doesn't run away. First, I trod on him, then Calder shot at him. Poor little guy must be traumatized."

"You think Calder is going to drop the charges?" Assaulting an officer of the law wasn't something to be taken lightly. Harding was going to skin me alive if I blew my cover. The SIA had planted enough backstory that any basic searches into Holly Day wouldn't reveal much, but if anyone were to dig deeper? Not good.

"He will if he knows what's good for him," Doris growled. "I threatened to report him for animal cruelty. And discharging his weapon."

"He's the sheriff. He's allowed to discharge his weapon."

The sound of booted feet and jingling keys had me pushing to my feet. Doris and I watched as Deputy Laura Biden approached, face blank. If I didn't know better, I'd think she was biting the inside of her cheek to stop from laughing.

No one said a word while Laura unlocked my cell.

"You're free to go," she said, swinging the door open and indicating with a wave of her arm that I could leave.

"And the charges?" Doris asked before I could get a word out.

"What charges?" Laura deadpanned.

"Yeah, thought so." Doris harrumphed, then linked her elbow with mine as we made our way out of the police station. Calder was nowhere to be seen, although one of the women who'd been at my house yesterday, the one who did cleaning as a job, was wiping down the front counter and watching us with wide eyes.

"Quit staring, Denise!" Doris snapped. Denise yelped and dropped her eyes, scrubbing harder at the counter.

"Let's go get some breakfast," Doris suggested once we were on the sidewalk. "All that excitement has given me an appetite."

"I could use a coffee," I agreed, following Doris to a

red 1962 Chevrolet Impala parked at the curb. "This is yours?"

"Sure is. Hop in." She slid behind the wheel, and I swear to God, standing at the hood, I could barely see the top of her head behind the steering wheel. I hurried as fast as possible to the passenger side and climbed in.

Doris was squinting through the steering wheel. I was not convinced she could see over the dash. "Can you even see to drive?"

"Only need my glasses for reading," she told me, turning the key in the ignition, shoving the transmission into reverse, and shooting backward out of the parking space without so much as a glance over her shoulder. She slammed on the brakes, ground the gears, then took off with a squeal of burning rubber.

Keeping one hand firmly gripping the door handle, I fumbled for my seat belt with the other. This five-foot-nothing of senior citizen drove like an absolute demon. I caught the terrified faces of the other motorists as Doris flew past them with barely an inch to spare before pulling the handbrake and skidding the car into a parking space not less than a hundred yards down the road.

"Here we are." She killed the engine. "River's."

"This is it? We could have walked." I glanced out the windshield at the café we'd just parked in front of. A large decal above the front awning read River's café-bakery-coffee. The building itself was cute and rustic, with patches of red brickwork strategically showing through the cream render.

"Holly Day, you seem to have forgotten you've got a busted foot." Doris shot me a look I couldn't read, then climbed out of the car, slamming the door with such force the whole car rocked. I followed at a slower pace. I shouldn't complain. Doris convinced Calder to drop the charges, and for that, I owed her.

"Don't worry, you're going to love River's. Best baked goods for miles around, but if you're one of those can't eat carbs types, she has other stuff too. Me? I'm partial to eggs and pancakes with two pieces of bacon."

My stomach rumbled at the mere mention of pancakes, reminding me that I'd spent the last twenty-four hours existing on nothing more substantial than coffee and a handful of health bars.

"Right now, I'd eat anything," I replied, following Doris through the door of River's. There was a scattering of tables, a row of booths along one wall, and above all else, a fabulous view across the bay. I automatically headed toward a window table, stopping to absorb the scene. The café was right on the beach. The sand and rocks were a brilliant hue of sand and sandstone. The sky was vivid and cloudless, and I felt like I was walking through a picture postcard. Heads swiveled to watch as we made our way across the café.

"This is amazing." I said it more to myself than to Doris, but she heard and beamed with pride.

"Gravestone may be small, but what we lack in population, we more than make up for with nature's beauty."

Windows and doors were propped open, letting the

cool sea breeze meander through the cafe, teasing my nostrils with the scent of seaweed, fish, and the ocean itself. Surprisingly, the fish smell wasn't bad, just fresh. A definite tang to the air, but a clean one. Not like the tang in the air when I'd first stepped into John Smith's home yesterday. That tang could only be described as putrid. I wrinkled my nose at the unpleasant memory.

"I smell fish," I said, taking my seat.

Doris pointed. "That'd be the old wharf. Locals fish off it."

I turned in my seat, spotting the old wooden structure that jutted out into the ocean. "Is it safe?" It didn't look safe. It looked like John's house. As if a strong wind would send the whole shebang tumbling into the ocean any second.

"Perfectly," Doris replied, picking up the menu and pretending to peruse it.

I did the same. Reading the selections available not only had my stomach rumbling even louder, but I was practically drooling. Now that I'd gotten used to the smells from the outside, the smells from inside, more importantly, the kitchen, now reached my nose and teased my appetite.

Which reminded me. "Doris? Any idea where I can get a new oven? Preferably delivered and installed?"

Doris eyeballed me over the top of her menu. "You cook?"

I shrugged and grinned self-consciously. "I bake." I hadn't baked in a long time, but being here in River's café, smelling all the wonderful baked goods and other delights, had suddenly reminded me that now was as good a time as any to indulge in one of my favorite pastimes of old.

"We'll drop by the hardware store after this. They can order you one in."

"Oh, good. I need some stuff from the hardware store anyway."

"Good morning, Doris," the server greeted us, order pad in hand. "I hear you were at the center of some excitement in town last night." News about the partial skeleton Flynn had found had traveled fast, it seemed, but then again, we were in a small country town. What else was there to talk about except for the skeleton that turned up the same day I did?

"River, I want you to meet Gravestone's newest resident, Holly Day. She's John Smith's great-niece." Doris beamed, and I bit back a smile. I had a feeling everyone here already knew exactly who I was. No introductions were necessary.

I looked up at the woman who sported short ginger hair cut in a pixie style, the bangs gently sweeping over a fresh, radiant face. Expressive green eyes sparkled at me as she smiled. Tattoos ran the length of one arm, and a medusa piercing sparkled as the diamond stud caught the light.

"Welcome, Holly. We'd about given up hope that John had any family left."

"Estranged. I didn't know about him until the lawyers tracked me down." I had a feeling River knew this anyway. Heck, I was sure Doris and her band of merry helpers had spread the word all over town that I was here to claim my inheritance. "This is your place, huh?"

River nodded. "I know it seems like hubris to name your business after yourself, but I originally started part-time out of my kitchen, and folks were used to going to River's for their baked goods, so when I expanded to an actual café, the name came with me." She turned her attention back to Doris. "I'm sure you have a theory as to who the bones belonged to?"

Doris fluttered her eyelashes and placed a hand on her chest. "Who, me? I couldn't possibly guess."

I snorted, and both women looked at me. "Sorry," I muttered, turning it into a cough.

"Word is you're saying it's Seth Saltzman," River persisted, and Doris shot her a steely glance.

"Lots of folks in this town wouldn't mind if that were the case. Including you."

River blanched. "He may be a low-down son of a bi —" She cut herself off and shot me an apologetic glance. "Sorry. While it was true I was angry with Seth, I wouldn't have killed him."

"So you say." Doris sniffed.

"Doris, surely you can't think I'd do such a thing?" River exclaimed, clearly distraught at the notion. "He was a two-timing weasel for sure, lower than a snake's belly in a wagon rut, but I did not harm one hair on that cheating man's head."

"You were… involved?" I asked.

"River was Seth's girlfriend. Well, the one in

Gravestone anyway," Doris supplied. "But she's right. I don't think she killed him."

River's shoulders slumped in relief. Curious that Doris's opinion of her held so much weight.

"Just remember, ladies, the bones haven't been identified. We don't know it was Seth Saltzman," I felt compelled to say. It was hardly fair of Doris to be accusing people of murder when we didn't even know who the victim was—or if they'd been murdered.

Doris made a grumbling noise and played with her menu.

River took the hint. "The usual?" she asked.

"Eggs and pancakes with two pieces of bacon," Doris declared, handing River her menu. "And a caramel latte."

"Holly?"

"I'll take Belgian waffles with butter and syrup. And an iced coffee."

"Coming right up." River took my menu and hurried off to fulfill our order, her steps light and fast as she wove her way through the café.

"She seems nice," I said, eyes drifting from River's departing back to the display case full of cakes, muffins, and desserts.

"One of Gravestone's success stories." Doris nodded. "Pretty much brought herself up, what with her alcoholic mom and deadbeat dad. When she disappeared to catering school, we thought we'd never see her again, that she'd left Gravestone in her rearview for greener pastures, but she proved us all wrong. Got herself qualified and came back home to set up her own business."

"It's nice to have a good news story every now and then. I have to say, this has inspired me to break out the baking pans."

"Probably need to buy some first," Doris teased.

"And ingredients." I sighed. "My shopping list is going to be huge." I did not want to think about the mammoth task ahead, so I brought the subject back to River. "You said River dated Seth?"

"Mmmhmm." Doris nodded, eyes on the sandy beach outside. Leading off the café was a deck with a smattering of tables with blue and white striped sun umbrellas. No one sat outside. It was already too hot for such foolishness. However, I imagined people would prefer to sit out there than indoors in the cooler months.

"And?" I prompted.

Doris turned her attention to me. The dreamy expression in her eyes cleared as she finally focused on what I was saying. "Oh, yes, right. She and Seth had been dating for…oh, I don't know, six months maybe?"

"And she didn't know about this other girl? The one he was seeing in Corpus Christi?"

Doris shook her head. "Nope. None of us did. So, of course, when the poor girl turned up, we were gobsmacked. At first, we marveled how a man with cancer had the stamina to be in a relationship with two women. I mean, chemo knocks you around. But of course, we quickly learned that the whole cancer thing was a big fat lie."

"How did River take it?"

"How do you think she took it?" Doris fiddled with the small vase sitting in the middle of the table that held a single yellow iris.

"Badly?" Badly enough to kill? *You don't even know if Seth is the victim*, I reminded myself.

"She was upset. She was also relieved he didn't have cancer. But hurt that he'd lied, not only to her but to everyone in Gravestone."

"And this other girl? What happened to her?"

Doris tapped her chin. "You know, I can't even remember her name...."

"Her name was Suzi." River set our drinks in front of us, swiveled on one heel, and stalked away without another word.

"Oops," Doris whispered, reaching for her latte. "Guess she overheard us."

Deciding a change in subject was in order, I grabbed a napkin, rummaged in my bag for a pen, and began my list in earnest, Doris chiming in with several totally unhelpful suggestions, such as a macrame potholder and a Nicholas Cage Shrek throw pillow.

CHAPTER
Seven

We didn't arrive back at John's house until just after one, the Impala laden with grocery bags. I'd ordered an oven and paid extra for it to be delivered and installed tomorrow. We'd stopped by Doris's house to grab fresh linen and towels, plus the pedestal fan she'd promised to loan me.

Things were coming together nicely, despite the rocky start to the day, and I was smiling as I limped up the front path, my already slow gait slowing further when I spied a note tacked to the front door. It wasn't until I'd climbed the two warped steps that I noticed what was sitting on the doorstep beneath the message.

"What the hell?" I backed up a step, then leaned over, peering at the skeletal hand that lay there. Straightening, I read the note.

"You weren't home, so I collected rubbish from out back. Call if you need anything further." It was signed Ken Opener, followed by a phone number. Pulling the note

from the door, I shoved it into my shorts pocket, making a note to ring and thank him and find out how much I owed.

"Holy heck, is that Seth's other hand?" Doris appeared behind me, a bag of groceries under each arm.

Wrestling the door open, I stepped over the hand and ushered Doris inside. "No. I think it's the same hand. Left. The question is, what is it doing on my doorstep?"

"Maybe Calder dropped it off? Maybe it's a fake or something?"

I glanced at her, noticed the flush of color in her cheeks and the way her eyes darted away. She was lying through her teeth. She knew as well as I did that the bones weren't fake.

Hands-on-hips, I tapped my good foot, demanding, "Okay, Doris. Spill. What do you know?"

"I know we should get the rest of the groceries out of the car before they spoil, and you should get rid of that hand before Calder comes looking for it," she said, stepping over the bones and returning to the car for the next load of groceries. She had a point. It wasn't going to look good for me if the sheriff turned up and found me in possession of the bones.

"Fine," I huffed, heading in search of a plastic bag. Doris had left behind the roll of garbage bags the day before, and I quickly snapped one off, returning to the front porch to snatch up the bones and wrap them in the plastic. The question was, where to hide them? My stomach churned like I'd eaten a box of ex-lax. The bones meant something, only what? And why did they return to me? Was it magic, or was it something else? Was someone messing with me? Planting evidence to force me to leave town?

I snorted out a laugh at my overactive imagination. Flynn appeared, paused to sniff the bones through the plastic, stood on his haunches for a moment while his nose twitched, and rubbed his paws over his face. He was rather adorable, I had to admit. And that's when I noticed something else.

"You've changed color!" I pointed at my once gray and white rat, who was now ginger and white.

Doris shoved past me, a bag of groceries under each arm. "Oh, you've got another rat. What's this one's name?"

"This is the same one." At least I was pretty sure this was Flynn. He still wore the leather harness. I squinted for a closer look. "You are Flynn, aren't you?"

He nodded, watching me watch him, no answers forthcoming on why his fur was now a different color. I scooped him up and held him up to my face. "What have you been up to, hmm?"

His whiskers twitched, and he rubbed his paws over his face. If only he could talk.

"Are you going to lend a hand, or are you going to gaze lovingly at your rat all day?" Doris inquired, sarcasm dripping from her words. "These groceries aren't going to unpack themselves."

"Sorry." Lowering Flynn to the floor, I hobbled to the bags vying for space on the counter. Unpacking the flour, sugar, baking powder, salt, cinnamon, more flour, and spices of almost every flavor, the shelves were soon bulging with baking ingredients, and a slither of excitement shot up my spine. Maybe I'd enjoy this enforced vacation after all. Once I'd solved the mystery of the bones, of course.

Doris was still coming and going, lugging in everything we'd managed to shove into the Impala and dumping it in my living room. I felt guilty that I couldn't help her, but the extra walking was making its presence felt in the throbbing of my broken foot. I refused to dwell on the fact that the medics couldn't heal me. I was a witch, and we healed fast naturally. Only, on this occasion? Not so much. Nope. Refused to dwell. It would be fine.

"Here." Doris threw a box at me, and I automatically caught it, staggering back a step to keep my balance. "Do something useful and get that going, would you?"

I grinned. "Now that, I can do." After unpacking the coffee maker, I had it set up within minutes. Flynn ran up my leg, gripped my shorts, and then leaped onto the counter, inspecting the remaining groceries.

"Do not be nibbling any holes in anything," I warned him, shaking my finger. "You will be amply fed, don't worry." Working around the rat, I slowly put away the rest of the groceries, thankful the ladies from yesterday had thoroughly cleaned everything, and I mean everything. Every shelf and every cupboard had been scrubbed. While they didn't precisely sparkle given their age and lack of maintenance up until this point, they did smell pleasantly of lemon. "Did you see who brought the bones back?" I asked Flynn.

He shook his head.

"That's even if they are the same bones. But what are the chances of two lots of skeletal remains turning up, and both left hands are found on my property?"

Flynn shrugged.

"And why on earth has your fur changed color?" I added. The bones thing was weird. The fur thing was even weirder.

"Maybe it was the fright he got when Calder shot at him," Doris suggested, dusting her hands together. "Everything's in," she added.

"Thanks, Doris, you've been such a help."

"Nonsense, it's what we small-town folks do."

My fingers stroked over the mark on my collarbone. "Doris, what you said earlier, before Flynn bit you and Calder shot at him...."

Doris's eyes dropped to the mark and then back up to my face. "Your birthmark?"

"You said it was a rune."

Her eyes shot to Flynn, then back to me. I glanced at the rat who was standing on his hind legs, front legs crossed over his chest, and if rats could frown, I'd say he was definitely frowning.

"Okay, spill." I crossed my own arms. "What's going on?"

"Ask him." Doris huffed, pointing at Flynn.

"I can't speak rat," I pointed out, then cocked my head. "Do you know why Flynn changed color?"

She shook her head. "No idea. But may I suggest we continue this conversation after we've hidden those bones? Because I suspect Calder is going to be beating down your door sometime soon, accusing you of taking them."

My eyebrows shot into my hairline. "Why would he accuse me of taking them? I was in the lockup!"

"You and I both know you didn't take them." Doris waved a hand as if to say the suggestion was ludicrous. "But you were there. In the vicinity. And you seem to have a good understanding of how lawmen think, how their minds work. Like it or not, you're a suspect."

"As are you. You were there too. I was the one locked up; you weren't. Maybe you had ample opportunity to slip into the evidence locker and snatch them." I glossed over the fact that she'd caught on to my knowledge of police procedures. One day in, and I was close to blowing my cover, to a little old lady no less.

Her eyes narrowed to mere slits. She didn't say anything, but the cogs were turning. Then her face cleared, and she smiled. "I didn't take them, and you didn't take them. This means the killer most likely took them and dumped them on your doorstep to try and implicate you somehow. Stupid plan. But regardless, Calder isn't likely to believe either of us."

I chewed my lip. "You're right. It sounds far-fetched. We need to hide the bones." The question was, where?

Standing beneath the cedar elm tree, I watched Doris shimmy her way up the trunk. Her idea of hiding the bones in the tree was actually pretty good, only I hadn't expected her to snatch them up, shove them into the back of her waist band, stick a roll of tape around her wrist like a bracelet, and practically sprint for the tree behind John's shed and begin climbing. By the time I'd reached the base of the trunk, she was halfway up.

"Doris, please be careful," I called, my heart skipping a beat watching this white-haired old lady climb the tree with remarkable ease. "I'm not sure it's safe for you to be up there."

"Have to go high enough that they won't be spotted from the ground," she shouted down at me.

"Don't fall," I yelled back.

"Roger."

Flynn scampered up behind her, which wasn't much of a comfort, for he wouldn't be able to stop her from falling, but at least she wasn't alone, and that, such as it was, *was* a comfort. I sighed, shaking my head. How had this become so complicated so fast? Who had taken the bones and left them on my doorstep? And why? It just didn't make sense.

I heard the sound of tape ripping and glanced up. I couldn't see Doris or the bones. "Everything okay?"

"Yep. Just taping them to this branch, so they don't fall down, then we're set." I imagined her wrapping Doris tape around and around the bones and the branch, the ripping sound a dead giveaway. Then I heard a grunt and a whispered, "Shit."

"What is it?"

"Nearly lost my dentures."

I frowned. "What? How?"

"Trying to bite through the tape. To cut it, you know?"

"Can't you just tear it with your fingers?"

"Nah. Need something sharper."

I thought for a moment, considered throwing a knife up to her, but if she caught it wrong, she'd either cut herself or fall out of the tree. A knife was not an option.

"Flynn? Can you assist?"

I thought I heard a squeak in response but couldn't be one hundred percent certain. A minute later, "By gads, he's done it. On my way down."

I didn't relax until Doris was back on solid ground, dusting off her blouse and pants. Flynn was on her shoulder, and she held up her hand to high-five him. "Thanks, Flynn." To my surprise, Flynn returned her high-five.

"You two friends now?" My eyes darted from Flynn to Doris and back again. Earlier, he'd bitten her. Now he was sitting on her shoulder exchanging high-fives. Today was not making sense.

Doris ignored my question and stood back, hands-on-hips, tilting her head back to peer up into the tree. Flynn mimicked her. I did, too, unable to stop myself.

"That's actually a pretty good hiding spot," I said. Even if the sheriff turned up with a warrant, he wouldn't think to search the tree.

Doris grinned and linked her elbow with mine, and

we slowly made our way back to the house. "Sometimes, I shock myself with the smart things I say and do," she said. "Then there are the times when I try to get out of the car with the seatbelt on."

I burst out laughing. I could totally see that being the case. We'd just stepped through the back door when we both heard it. A car pulling up out front. No bets on who it could be.

"Show time," Doris said, patting her hair. "How do I look?"

I plucked a leaf from her hair and shoved it in my pocket, straightened her blouse, and smoothed my hands over her shoulders. "Not like you just climbed a tree," I said with a nod.

"How's that coffee coming along?" She nodded to the machine that I'd set up earlier, and while I was busy pouring us both a cup, Calder hammered on the front door. Doris called, "I'll get it!" and I couldn't help the grin at our subterfuge.

"You still here?" Calder barked.

"As you can see, Sheriff," Doris replied. I stilled, listening in. She'd called him Sheriff. What did that mean, if anything? That he was pissed? I'd bet he was.

"May I come in?" His voice sounded like he'd been chewing nails. Definitely pissed. The hinges on the front door squawked their protest as Doris opened the door wider, ushering him inside.

"Coffee?" I called from the kitchen, looking up when he appeared in the doorway.

"Where are they?" he demanded, jaw clamped, pulse ticking in the vein at his temple.

"Where are what?" I played dumb, holding out a cup to Doris, who took it from me and sat at the kitchen table, settling in to watch how this would play out.

"The bones," he snapped. "They were at the station. Now they're not. Where are they?"

I flattened a hand against my chest and gasped, eyes wide. "Why, Sheriff, are you telling me you lost evidence?" I looked down at Doris. "Are the bones actually evidence? They're human remains, so that would make them… the victim?"

Doris nodded like a bobblehead. "You're right!"

"Enough!" Calder barked. If he clenched his jaw any tighter, he'd break some teeth. "You were at the station." He pointed an accusing finger at me. "You had the opportunity."

I refrained from saying to Doris *I told you so*. "I was in your lockup," I pointed out. "How, pray tell, would I manage to steal the bones? And have you stopped to ask yourself why I would even want to? I have absolutely zero motive, Sheriff, and yet here you are, accusing me of a heinous crime."

He reached into his pocket and pulled out a crumpled piece of paper, slapping it down on the kitchen counter. "I have a warrant to search the premises."

Doris gasped, her hand clutching her neck. "Calder!" she admonished. "Leave the poor girl alone. She didn't take your precious bones."

He pinned her with a glare. "I'm searching your house next, Doris, so I suggest you pipe down."

"Well, I never!" she declared, fanning her face.

"Pretty quick off the draw with that warrant." I picked it up and gave it a cursory glance. "You really didn't need to go to all that trouble. I'd have happily let you look around if only you'd asked." I blinked and batted my lashes, doing my best to convey my utter innocence.

"Why do I get the feeling you're toying with me?" He relaxed a fraction, his jaw unclenching.

"I don't know, why?"

He sighed a heartfelt sigh that went all the way down to his toes. He rubbed a hand around his neck, then looked at me. "That offer of coffee still stand?"

I smiled brightly. My face almost cracked. "Sure."

CHAPTER
Eight

Calder did not find the bones. Doris and I agreed we'd leave them in the tree until we figured out what to do about them. Maybe we could hand them in later, say we found them, again. For Calder to get a search warrant meant he didn't trust me, and who could blame him? I was new to town. An unknown entity. It was much easier for him to think I was capable of doing such a thing than a local he knew and trusted. But still, the fact remained that someone had taken those bones from the sheriff's office and left them on my doorstep. And that someone had managed to do it in broad daylight without anyone noticing.

Doris left shortly after Calder, with instructions to call her should anything happen. I'm not sure what she was expecting to happen, but I had my fingers crossed for a peaceful evening. Exhaustion was pulling at me. I'd hardly slept the night before, but now that I had a fan and a few more home comforts, I was planning on turning in early to get some much-needed sleep. No sooner had I thought it than a knock sounded at the front door.

I was expecting it to be either Calder or Doris. But when I opened the door, a stranger was standing there. Middle-aged, mouse-brown hair cut so short I could see his scalp, gut hanging over the belt of his jeans, faded red plaid shirt hanging open over a stained white T-shirt. The unmistakable tang of body odor emanated from him.

"Yes?" I kept one hand on the door, the other on the jamb, preventing him from stepping inside. Not that he tried. He looked over one shoulder, then the other, in what could only be described as a furtive manner, then leaned forward. "Is John here?"

"I'm sorry. John died."

"Died? Tell him it's Steve."

"Steve, John passed away. I can't tell him anything."

Steve looked over his shoulder again. "Sure, okay, whatever. Who are you again?"

"I'm Holly. John was my great uncle."

"Holly, huh? Holly… yeah, Holly, I think John mentioned you."

My eyes narrowed. "I doubt it, but go ahead. How can I help?"

"I dropped by to make sure the thing is still on for Friday?" Steve said in hushed tones, again glancing over his shoulder as if expecting someone to be there, listening. I looked over his shoulder myself, but there was nothing but darkness and the faint glow of the lone street light farther down the block.

"What thing?"

"The thing, you know."

"I don't know, Steve."

"Well, yeah, I know you don't know, but is it on?"

"I have no idea what you're talking about." I was starting to think Steve had a mental issue, possibly dementia, and had wandered off from wherever it was he was supposed to be.

"Okay, I get it. Of course, you don't know. But, all I'm saying is, we're good, right?"

"We are not good, Steve. I don't know what you're talking about."

"Of course. Got it. No idea. Great. Friday?"

"Steve, John is no longer alive, so whatever you think is happening on Friday is not happening. Understand?"

"Perfectly. Tell him I'll see him then." Steve hurried away, and I watched him leave. No vehicle—he'd arrived on foot. Shaking my head, I closed the door, locking it in case Steve decided to return looking for John.

"Today has been all kinds of weird," I said to Flynn as I lay down on my camp bed, fully clothed. I was too tired to shower, change, and do anything other than lay here and let sleep claim me.

Flynn made a chittering noise that I took as agreement. My eyes drifted shut, and I listened as Flynn settled himself on the camp chair, his claws scratching at the canvas fabric. Doris had set up the pedestal fan, and the breeze swept over me in intervals as the fan oscillated from side to side. I could get up and adjust it, so it blew on me constantly, but that took too much effort. An intermittent breeze was better than no breeze, and that was my last thought before sleep claimed me.

I must've slept like the dead because the next thing I knew, there was a weight on my chest and a pounding at my front door. I was in the same position I'd fallen asleep in, flat on my back, still clothed, walking boot still on.

Four little feet dug into my chest, and I peered down to see Flynn standing on me.

"Did you sleep there all night?" I ground out. My morning breath hit him full force in the face, and his nose screwed up, and he raised both paws to cover his face, turning his head away in disgust. "Serves you right," I grumbled, dislodging him as I sat up.

The knock came again. "Okay, okay, I'm coming!" I yelled. Heaving myself off the cot, I ran my fingers through my hair and limped to the door, knowing full well I looked a red hot mess. I briefly wondered who my visitor could be. Steve from last night? Doris? Or Calder?

It was none of them. I blinked in shock, my eyes wandering over the six-foot built to perfection man standing on my doorstep. His hair was that color in between blond and brunette. What did they call that? Dirty blond? It was cut short but with enough length to invite a girl to run her fingers through it. Strong jaw, tanned skin, sapphire blue eyes, and a body that showed he took care of it.

"Holly?" he asked, one brow raised.

Suddenly conscious of my morning breath, I turned my head to the side. "That's me. Who are you?"

"Matt Casey." He held out a hand, and I automatically shook it, noting he had the perfect handshake—not too firm, not too limp. Although I highly doubted anything about Matt Casey could be described as limp. "Gravestone's handyman and carpenter. I'm here to install your new oven."

"Oh!" My heart skipped a beat, excitement cascading through my veins. Not only was I getting my new oven, but I was getting what could only be described as eye-candy installing it for me. Maybe my luck was changing.

"Okay if I come in? I'll need to remove the old oven first."

"Sure, sure. Sorry, I'm not quite awake yet."

"Not sleeping well, huh? Not surprising, really. The mangroves can be pretty spooky if you're not used to the noises."

"That and this house. It groans more than an old woman." I preceded him into the kitchen and waved at the offending stove. "It's all yours. I'm going to take a quick shower. You okay on your own?"

"Absolutely. Take your time." He was already wriggling the filthy old oven out from between the cupboards. "I'll just get my toolbox, so I can get this beast unhooked."

"Sure." I was already at the foot of the stairs. My foot was itching like crazy, probably because I'd had the walking boot on for twenty-four hours straight, and all the sweat and dirt had accumulated, not only gross but irritating my skin. My suitcase was still in the spare bedroom, and I dug around inside for clean underwear, shorts, and this time, a soft, oversized cotton blouse in a pale blue with big white polka dots.

I wiped down the walking boot with a damp cloth in the bathroom, wrinkling my nose at the smell, before leaving it to dry outside the bathroom door. Stepping beneath the spray, I heaved a heartfelt sigh as the water sluiced over me, washing away the dried sweat and grime of the previous day. I took longer in the shower than I usually would, standing under the needles of water pondering the mysterious bones and what it all meant. The rest of the body hadn't been found, making me think the bones had washed up in the mangroves. If Sheriff Josh Calder was an intelligent man—and I thought he was—he'd start searching the mangroves for the rest of the remains.

But that still didn't explain who had stolen them from the police station and left them on my doorstep. If they wanted to implicate me, leaving them on the doorstep was a stupid plan. Or were they meant to be a warning? A *you're next* type of thing? And was the visit from crazy guy Steve last night purely coincidence, or was it connected? I was also beyond curious about what 'uncle' John got up to on Fridays.

With no answers forthcoming, I turned off the taps

and stepped out of the shower, wrapping a towel around myself. The door inched forward a fraction, and Flynn slipped inside. Only this time, his fur was entirely black. He still wore the leather harness, so it had to be him… unless I had an infestation of rats that all wore harnesses.

"Flynn?" I figured I should probably check.

He sat on his haunches and nodded.

"Right. What is it with the color changes?" I asked. He shrugged. I shooed him out of the bathroom, telling him I'd see him downstairs when I was dressed. Quickly drying myself off, I combed my hair and left it loose to dry, slipped into my shorts and blouse, strapped the cumbersome walking boot back on, and made my way downstairs, my nose following the blissful scent of coffee.

On my kitchen bench was a steaming mug, the old oven was out, and the new range was sitting in the middle of the kitchen, Matt tearing off the cardboard packaging.

"Oh, hey, I made you a coffee. Hope that's okay?"

I picked up the mug and took a sip. "That's more than okay; it's encouraged," I said. "I hope you made one for yourself?"

"Sure did." He jerked his head toward the sink, where another cup sat. Matt stopped what he was doing and dragged one of the chairs toward me. "Here. Sit. Rest that foot."

Taken aback, I did, watching as he grabbed the second chair and positioned it in front of me, gently lifting my injured foot and propping it on the chair. "Okay?" he inquired.

"Fine. Thank you." I wasn't used to someone taking care of me, but I had to admit I could certainly get used to someone as cute as Matt Casey stepping up for the role. I decided to ignore the fact that I was ten years, if not more, older than him.

"So, Matt," I began, but he interrupted, "Call me Casey. Everyone does."

"Okay, Casey," I said. "You said you're a carpenter? While you're here, do you think I could get a quote for fixing up this place?"

Casey froze, his blue eyes flashing. "You're staying?"

I shrugged. "Maybe. But if not, then I'll sell, and to be perfectly honest, I'd probably have to pay someone to take it in its current condition."

Casey stood with his hands on his hips and surveyed the room. "Needs a lot of work."

"I know."

"Did you know your uncle built this place?"

"Great uncle," I corrected automatically.

"And that he was a carpenter himself?"

"I'd heard that, yes. What's your point?"

"That, structurally, this place is probably pretty sound."

"But you'll check to make sure, right?"

"Of course." He turned his attention back to unpacking the oven. "I have another job straight after this. Joan is renovating her laundry. It should only take a couple of days."

"Okay."

"Then I'll come back and measure up and prepare a quote for you. In the meantime, think about what you want."

"I want it to look good."

He grinned. "Besides that. Are you thinking of knocking any walls down, opening this place up?" He jerked his thumb at the wall between the living room and kitchen.

I chewed my lip, considering my options. He had a point. If I took out that wall and made the living room and kitchen open plan, that'd make it so much bigger. A plus for potential buyers.

"Just make a wish list," Casey continued, "and I'll let you know how much it'll cost. If it's out of your budget, then we'll adjust."

I narrowed my eyes. "You don't want to know my budget first?" Was I about to get scammed? I hoped not. I kinda liked Casey. Well, I liked the way he looked, as shallow as that sounds. It would be a major bummer if he ripped off his clients.

"Either way, I'm easy." He shrugged. "I can do the bare minimum, or we can go all out, or somewhere in between. It's up to you." He'd finished stripping the packaging from the oven and carted it out to his truck, telling me he'd dispose of it for me, that it was all part of the service. When he came back, he had a thoughtful expression on his face.

"I hear you found… human remains here?"

"Well, my pet rat did."

Casey's eyes rounded. "You have a pet rat?"

"Yeah, I'm surprised you haven't seen him." I looked around for Flynn, but he wasn't in the kitchen. "Flynn!" I called. A minute later, tiny paws came pitter-pattering into the kitchen, and the now midnight black rat scampered to my side, climbed up the side of the chair, and sat on my lap.

"This is Flynn. Flynn, this is Casey." I introduced them.

Casey was nodding his head. "A pet rat. Well, I never."

"You're not afraid of him?"

Casey looked puzzled. "Scared of a rat? No. Why would I be?"

I shrugged, mouth turning down. "Oh, no reason. Just that the sheriff is. He tried to shoot him."

Casey threw back his head and laughed out loud. "Yeah, Calder has one weakness. Unfortunately for Flynn, that weakness is rodents."

Casey came across and stroked his fingers down Flynn's back. "His fur is so soft!"

"Right?" I agreed.

Casey crouched by my side, bringing himself eye level with Flynn. "So, you found some bones, hey, buddy?"

Flynn nodded, and I tensed. Did I need to remind him that he was meant to pretend that he was an actual rat and not a shifter trapped in rat form?

"Did he just nod?" Casey looked up at me. I could see flecks of turquoise in his blue eyes at this range. They really were quite stunning, his lashes dark and thick, framing them perfectly.

"He does that," I lied. "He'll nod to pretty much anything you say."

Casey bought my explanation for Flynn's unusual behavior and straightened, returning to the oven.

"Any idea who the bones belonged to?" he asked, grunting as he maneuvered the oven back into the space the previous one had occupied.

"I have no idea since I'm new in town. But Doris mentioned Seth Saltzman. Apparently, he disappeared a while back, but that's purely speculation."

Casey glanced at me over his shoulder. "Seth, huh? Makes sense."

"Why's that?"

"Well, if anyone deserved a sticky end, it was him."

"Oh?" I played dumb. "You knew him?"

"Everyone knew him. He was a fraud and a charlatan."

"Charlatan? How so?"

Casey paused, his jaw hardening, and his eyes taking on a steely glow. "He stole River from me. He's a home wrecker."

I blinked in surprise. Doris hadn't mentioned River had been dating Casey. "What happened?" I pressed, eager to learn more about Seth Saltzman and his womanizing ways.

"River and I had been dating since high school,"

Casey said in a rush. "And yeah, okay, so things weren't perfect, but I never thought Seth would make a move on her! Here I was, thinking we were happy, that everything was okay, and the next thing, she's telling me it's over, that she's met someone else."

Ouch. Not that I had a lot of experience with heartache since I never let myself get involved, but I'd imagine that sort of betrayal would hurt.

"So, she dumped you for Seth," I repeated, remembering what Doris had told me at River's bakery, that River and Seth had dated for six months or so before the whole town had discovered his scam—and the other girlfriend he had squirreled away in Corpus Christi.

"Guess her judgment was way off," he grumbled, wiping his palms on his jeans. "Turns out Seth was cheating on her with some girl in Corpus Christi. And he lied about having cancer. The whole town wanted blood over that one."

"After Seth disappeared, did you and River resolve your differences?"

"You mean did we get back together? No. She was right. We'd both changed. I'm only sorry it was Seth who was the catalyst and that she ended up getting hurt. I only want good things for her, for her to be happy."

Casey returned to working on the stove, and I continued to study him, one part of me admiring his male form while the other pondered if he was capable of murder. Did he kill Seth Saltzman in retaliation for stealing his girl? But why wait until they'd split up? If he was that cut up about it, wouldn't he kill him straight away? But maybe the catalyst was when it was revealed that Seth had not only lied about his cancer but that he'd been cheating on River the whole time. Casey could have killed him as a chivalrous act.

Which brought me back to the question… was Matt Casey capable of murder?

CHAPTER
Nine

I t was midday by the time Casey left. I was pretty sure he'd stretched out that last hour, taking his time fussing with the oven, and my ego inflated considerably that he was dragging his heels just to spend time with me. Until he burst my bubble by explaining that Joan Jackson, the laundry renovation client, would not be home until lunchtime. Something about the Women of Gravestone Committee meeting and that if he timed it right, he could go straight from one job to the other.

After watching him leave, I returned to the kitchen, running my hand over my new oven. I really wanted to bake, but it was as hot as hades. I'd have to wait until evening before I fired this baby up, but I was mentally preparing what delights I'd produce. Snickerdoodle's, apple fritters, all kinds of fruit cobblers.

A movement out the kitchen window caught my eye, and I leaned over the sink to peer through the dirty glass. *Really must get around to cleaning the windows. Maybe I could hire Denise to come clean them?*

There! In the mangroves… was that an arm? Waving?

Stepping onto the back deck, I carefully made my way down the steps and through the trampled weeds, my hand shielding my eyes from the blazing sun as I cautiously approached the mangroves. Then I spotted her. In a flat bottomed boat, hidden amongst the mangroves, was Doris.

"Oh good, you saw me." She smiled. Today, she was wearing a leopard print blouse accompanied by olive green waders. A fisherman's hat, complete with fishing hooks attached to the brim, perched on her white hair.

"What on earth are you doing?" I asked. Doris had hold of an overhead branch while she sat perched on one of the bench seats in the tin boat.

"We're going looking for the rest of Seth's body!" she declared. She waved me forward. "Hop in, hop in."

I eyed the small boat, the front end wedged into the mangroves while Doris held it in place. "I'm not sure I can. Don't want to get my walking boot wet."

"Easily fixed." To my horror, Doris threw a leg over the side of the boat and stepped out. That's when I discovered the water was less than a foot deep. Now I understood the waders. "They're going to build a boardwalk out here," she said while moving to the back of the boat where an outboard motor was attached. She started pushing the boat closer to the shore where I stood. "Some eco-tourism type thing."

"A boardwalk?" I looked over my shoulder to where my house stood, not far from the mangroves.

"Mmhmm. John was vehemently opposed to it. Said it was an invasion of his privacy, what with the mangroves right on his boundary. But now he's dead, there's no one to oppose it. I'm guessing the Council will move fast."

"And what do the neighbors think?" I looked toward my neighbor's house, hidden behind a row of trees. Once I was more settled, I'd go over and introduce myself.

"Oh, that house is empty. Has been for years. Council wants it demolished. John's place too. Kerris was fit to explode when she heard you'd arrived. I think she was hoping to grab the place for a song in an estate sale and bulldoze the lot."

"Kerris?"

"Kerris Jones, Gravestone's Mayor." A shudder went through Doris's body. "Can't trust her as far as you could throw her. Which wouldn't be far on accounting of her size."

Doris finally succeeded in maneuvering the boat, so all I had to do was climb in over the front. Throwing my injured leg in first, I pushed off with my good foot, the momentum shoving the boat backward with a sudden jolt. I lost my balance and catapulted forward, landing in a heap in the bottom. Doris shrieked, the boat slamming into her. I saw her mouth make the perfect O before she disappeared from view with a splash.

"Doris!" Scrambling as fast as I could, which wasn't

easy with the boat rocking in what little water it had, I made my way to the rear of the boat. I peered over the edge to find Doris sitting in the water, laughing her head off. Lucky for her, the waders reached her armpits, and the water didn't.

"I'm so sorry," I said, holding out my hand to help her to her feet. She took it, and we managed to get her into the boat amongst much giggling. Finally settling on the front bench while Doris took the back, she yanked the motor's pull cord, and the engine roared to life.

"How come I didn't hear you approach?" I asked over the noise of the motor.

"Because I didn't want you to," was her cryptic answer. "Duck!" she yelled.

"Where?" I turned my head to look for the feathered critter and instead got whacked in the forehead with an overhanging branch. The boat's momentum, traveling in the opposite direction, was enough to knock me off my seat, and I was once more in the bottom of the boat, this time flat on my back.

"Why didn't you duck?" Doris asked, puzzled as to why I hadn't avoided the branch.

"Because I thought you meant duck, as in a bird!" I pushed myself back up and onto my seat, this time keeping an eye out for low-hanging branches. My forehead was throbbing, and a gentle probe with my fingers told me I had a large egg forming. I was going to be covered in bruises before the day was out.

Doris kept the throttle low, and we slowly weaved in and around the mangroves. I kept my eyes trained on the roots and bases of the trees, anywhere a body would likely get caught up, while Doris focused on not crashing us into those roots and trees.

"Hold it right there!" A voice echoed across the water, unnaturally loud.

I practically jumped out of my skin. Turning, I saw Calder in a similar boat to ours, only bigger, with a megaphone held to his mouth.

"Uh-oh," Doris muttered before yelling at the sheriff, "What's that, Calder? Can't hear you over the engine."

"Turn your engine off, Doris," Calder drawled, still using the loud speaker. "I'm coming alongside."

"Busted," she said beneath her breath. I looked at her, wide-eyed.

"Are we not supposed to be in the mangroves?" I whispered, trying not to move my lips. "Is this off-limits?"

Doris snorted. "Of course not. Anyone can enjoy the mangroves."

I relaxed. "What's the problem then?"

Doris dutifully killed the engine, and Calder brought his boat alongside.

"The problem is Doris doesn't have a boat license," he said, having overheard.

My brows shot up. "You need a boat license? That's a thing?"

"It's a thing," Calder confirmed. To Doris, he said, "Does Mary Lou know you have her boat?"

"I only borrowed it," Doris huffed. "I'm going to put it back."

I couldn't contain my eye roll. Great. Now I was aiding and abetting a boat thief.

"Care to explain what you're doing out here?" Calder asked, resting one arm on his knee where his foot was propped on the side of his boat. I got the sense he'd had this conversation with Doris more than once.

"I'm showing Holly the sights." Doris grinned. I looked around. The mangroves were scenic enough. I supposed it wasn't a bad excuse as far as excuses went.

"Is that right?" Calder drawled. "So, you wouldn't be out here searching for missing bones?"

"Nope," Doris shot back. "But if we happen to come across them, we'll be sure to let you know."

"Any word on who took the hand?" I asked. "Does the station have CCTV?"

Calder straightened. "This isn't CSI. We have no need for CCTV." His tone suggested he didn't appreciate my inquiry.

"Seems to me it sure would come in handy for finding out who walked into your station, in broad daylight, and helped themselves to evidence. Without anyone noticing." I couldn't resist the barb. It still stung that he'd immediately suspected it was me and had a search warrant issued post haste. That search warrant meant my name, well, my alias's name, was now in the system. Not an ideal situation.

He smiled—one of those patronizing, fake smiles. "Stay out of this investigation. Both of you. If I discover you poking your noses in, you'll find yourselves back in the cells."

"Is that a threat?"

"It's a promise." His voice, edged with steel, brooked no argument, so I was totally disarmed when he winked, then shoved his booted foot against the side of our boat, separating the two vessels. "Get Mary Lou's boat back to her right this minute Doris, before she reports it stolen. Again." With that, he revved his engine and powered away, leaving our little boat rocking in his wake. I gripped the sides, white-knuckled until the water settled.

"Guess we'd better do as he says," I said, but Doris just laughed at me.

"We've got as much right to be out on the water as anyone else," she declared.

"But apparently, you need a boat license, Doris. Which you don't have. So the sheriff, on this occasion, has a point." I didn't mention the small matter of her stealing the boat.

She cocked her head, considered my words, and eventually nodded, her shoulders slumping in defeat. "Fine. Didn't peg you for a spoilsport."

My brows shot up. "And I didn't peg you as a boat thief."

Before I could argue further, she twisted the throttle, and the boat shot forward, cutting off any further conversation.

Once we cleared the mangroves, Doris drove us out into the bay, and I had to admit, it was beautiful.

Pristine beaches, a tree-lined shore, and historic buildings against a backdrop of rolling farmlands and hills presented a picturesque setting for the charming town of Gravestone. Out on the water, the ocean breeze was cooling, taking the edge off the heat of the day.

"It's beautiful," I sighed, seeing Gravestone from a whole new perspective.

"What's that?" Doris yelled, then killed the engine, letting us float with the current.

"I said it's beautiful." I swiveled on my seat, half facing Doris, half facing the town.

"It sure is." Doris beamed.

"Have you lived here long?"

"All my life."

I couldn't begin to imagine living in one place for your entire life. I never stayed in one spot for longer than three months, sometimes six depending on the job and how deep undercover I had to go. This was the first time in my adult life that I was forced to take time off, and while I had a couple of projects to keep me occupied, I honestly wasn't sure how long I'd be able to stand being cooped up in Gravestone, unable to work. It's not that I didn't like the town. I did. It was the work aspect.

"Oh, heck," Doris muttered. "There's Mary Lou's car. Better get the boat back."

Before I could respond, Doris pulled the rip cord, and the outboard motor roared to life. She twisted the throttle and spun the boat around. I sat in the middle and gripped either side of the boat with white knuckles while she raced toward the shore. I spotted River's and the old jetty. Doris shot past the end of the jetty and then turned a sharp left, revealing a boat ramp. An olive green Land Rover was parked on the boat ramp with a boat trailer attached, partially submerged.

"Hold tight!" Doris yelled, lining the boat up with the trailer.

"What?" I screeched. "No way! Doris, you can't drive the boat right onto the trailer!" I cried, horrified that I was most definitely facing my impending death. The tide had clearly receded since Doris had launched the boat. There was not enough water to get the boat back onto the trailer. Not without reversing the trailer farther down the boat ramp, which would have been the sensible thing to do. I considered offering to do it myself; it wouldn't kill me to take off my boot and wade through the water to the jeep. But Doris was having none of it. In the mere seconds I'd had to think of another, more sensible approach, the distance between us and the trailer was nonexistent.

Doris cut the engine. I lowered my chin to my chest and squeezed my eyes shut, kissing my butt goodbye. Who knew I'd go out in a vehicle versus boat accident in small-town Texas? With my jaw clamped so tight my teeth ached, I waited for the impact. There was a jolt, the sound of metal scraping against steel, then nothing. We were stationary. Prying open one eye, then the other, I looked around in disbelief. She'd done it! The boat was safely on the trailer. We hadn't plowed through the back of the

Land Rover. There was no shattered glass or mangled metal. *We were alive!*

Doris hopped out and attached the boat to the trailer at the front, explaining that Mary Lou kept her boat and its trailer at the boat ramp three hundred and sixty-five days a year, which, in Doris's opinion, meant she didn't mind if people borrowed it. After all, there was nothing stopping anyone from doing exactly what Doris had done—reversed the trailer to the boat ramp and taken the boat for a spin.

The Land Rover's door slammed, then the engine roared to life, and Doris towed the trailer out of the water, expertly maneuvering to reverse park it in the parking lot. Winding down her window, she leaned out and yelled, "Hop out here. I'll finish up and meet you up at River's. You okay to walk that far?"

"Sure." River's was on the other side of the jetty, which conveniently hid the boat ramp—and Doris's thievery—from view. It was a tad challenging to climb out of the boat while it was atop the trailer, especially with a walking boot, but I managed it and hobbled my way up the incline toward the shore and River's bakery. A few minutes later, the Land Rover roared past me. Doris gave a quick toot on the horn and a wave out the window, then turned in the opposite direction to River's.

"Oh, my God," I whispered to myself, watching the departing Land Rover. "Did she steal that too?"

A few short minutes later, I reached River's at the same time Doris did, the roar of her red Impala impossible to miss. I stood at the entrance, hand shielding my eyes, and waited for her. I'd left home without my purse, phone, or anything. I hadn't been expecting to need any of those things. I'd also left home without locking up, which rankled because I wasn't usually that careless.

"Oh, hi, Holly." Doris waved, having exchanged her waders for a pair of bright yellow pants. "Fancy seeing you here."

"Fancy," I drawled. "I take it that Land Rover wasn't yours?"

"Gus O'Genn's." She winked. "He wasn't using it."

"Did he even know you borrowed it?"

"Does it even matter?" She darted in front of me and opened the door, preceding me inside. I had a funny feeling hanging out with Doris for any length of time was going to see me spending more time in Sheriff Calder's cells. I smiled, the first honest to God smile I'd smiled in a long time, and followed Doris inside.

"Ladies." River looked up from behind the counter. "Lunching out today?"

Doris glanced at me, and I shrugged. "May as well." Despite having a kitchen stocked with groceries and a new, functioning oven, we were here now, and the truth was, I was hungry.

We sat at the same table near the window as yesterday. "I don't think I could ever get tired of this view." I sighed, cupping my chin in my hand and gazing at the ocean.

"Word is you cut the Women's meeting before it had finished, Doris?" River laid two menus on the table and waited for Doris's explanation as to why she'd missed the meeting. Whatever it was. I half-listened, keeping most of my attention on the view.

"Didn't miss anything important, I bet." Doris sniffed with disdain. "Ever since Kerris elbowed her way in, she's run the meetings as an extension of the Council. All to forward her own agenda."

"I admit I've only ever been to one or two in the past, but they were great. Very entertaining," River replied. "You're not the first person who's told me they've changed."

"What is this meeting anyway?" I asked.

"It's the Women of Gravestone Committee," Doris said. "We meet every month to discuss how we can help each other and plan any upcoming events."

"Help each other how?"

"There was one time when Myra hadn't pooped in a week. Poor girl was fit to burst. She'd tried everything. Everything," Doris said. "So, we all put our heads together to come up with a solution."

"I don't think I want to know what the solution was," I muttered, and River grinned.

"I remember that," she said. "Myra ended up in the hospital."

"What?" I gasped, eyes round. "Now I want to know."

Doris waved a hand to shush me. "Nonsense. That's not important. What is important is that Kerris, who never bothered to attend before she was mayor, decided we were to become her committee. Next thing you know, she's got us on work detail, cleaning the public toilets, litter duty in the park, running fundraisers for her mayoral campaign."

"Why don't you kick her out?"

Doris's eyes narrowed, mired in the memory. "We tried. But it has to go to a vote, majority rules. So, we voted, and she won. So, she stays. And she made herself chairwoman. So, now she sets the rules."

River looked surprised. "She won the vote?"

Doris folded her arms over her chest. "Yep. I have no doubt she had something over those women who voted for her. She has a way of learning your secrets and using them against you."

"She doesn't sound very nice," I said, perusing the menu. "You should start your own committee."

Utter silence met my words, and I glanced up to see River and Doris staring at me, astonished. "What?" I protested. "Is there a law in Gravestone that you can only have one women's committee? If so, don't call it a committee. Call it a club or a group or anything else, really. Ladies, you have options." I couldn't believe they hadn't thought of this themselves.

River turned to Doris. "You know, we could…."

"We really could," Doris agreed.

"There'd have to be rules."

"Of course."

"A sure-fire way to keep Kerris out."

"That's easy," I cut in. "No council members. Mayor or not, you don't want anyone reporting back to her on what you're up to."

"You are a genius." Doris reached over and patted my hand.

I shrugged. "Not really. But thanks."

The bell above the front door jingled, and River turned to see a group of workmen enter. "Uh-oh, lunch crowd is about to hit." She jerked her thumb toward the men. "This is the crew working on the road into town."

"We'd better order and let you get back to it," I said. "I'll have the Florentine paninis and a coffee. Long black."

"I'll have the Texas Wave paninis and a caramel latte," Doris said.

River scribbled down our orders, collected the menus, and departed with the promise that our food wouldn't take long.

"Casey mentioned the Gravestone Women's Committee this morning," I said. "He was killing time before he had to go to a job at Joan Jackson's. Said she would be at the meeting."

"Matt Casey was at your house?" Doris asked with an unmistakable twinkle in her eye.

"Yeah. He was installing my new oven. He's coming back to give me a quote on some repairs around the place. Why?"

Doris leaned forward, elbows on the table, and stage whispered, "Casey and River used to be a thing."

"Yeah. He told me. High school sweethearts."

"Until Seth Saltzman came along." Doris's brow furrowed, the lines deep in her tanned skin.

Out of all the empty tables, the workmen chose to sit directly behind us, their voices loud as they settled into their seats, laughing and riling each other, making conversation impossible. Rather than try to shout over their raucousness, I turned my attention to the view once more, hypnotizing myself watching the waves wash upon the shore, the men's voices nothing but background noise. Only my training meant I was never switched off. My ears pricked up when one of them mentioned the track they'd found. The one that had been intentionally hidden. When they finished resealing the road, they planned to go back and check it out and see what was at the end.

My eyes met Doris's. She'd heard it too. We had to be thinking the same thing.

"We need to check that out," I said.

"We can call ourselves Keen Agers," she said.

"What?" we said in unison.

"What are you talking about?" I jumped in before she could speak again.

"Our new women's committee. We can call ourselves Keen Agers. What are you talking about?"

I jerked my thumb behind us. "This lot found a hidden road. I say we check it out."

She leaned back, frowning. "Why? That doesn't sound very exciting."

My brows shot up. "No? A secret road? Intentionally hidden? A missing body? You don't think those two things might be connected?"

"Oh!" Realization dawned. "You're right."

"Usually am."

"Modest too."

"I've been accused of worse."

Doris laughed out loud, drawing the attention of the

men at the table behind us. Doris flirted up a storm with the men, and before I knew it, we had the location of the hidden track they'd unearthed. Then our food arrived, putting an end to the banter.

"How'd you do that?" I lowered my voice so the men wouldn't overhear.

"Do what?"

"Charm them so easily?"

"I've had years of practice, child." Doris winked. "That and a little magic."

My brows shot up. "Magic?"

"Mmm. You know." Doris wriggled her fingers. "A little razzle-dazzle."

"Riiggghhhht." Usually, I could peg people straight away, but Doris remained an enigma. There was more to her than met the eye, that was for sure, and I pondered the old woman and her insane level of fitness while I ate my panini.

"Urgh," Doris grumbled, dabbing at her mouth with a paper napkin, her eye on the door and who'd just walked in.

I glanced over to see a tall, overweight woman step inside. She wore a tweed skirt with a matching jacket that was incongruent with the current temperature. The navy pumps on her feet appeared to be two sizes too small, given the amount of flesh squeezing over the top. A long string of pearls bounced on her ample bosom while she slid a pair of oversized sunglasses down her nose, surveying the room.

"Who's that?" I asked.

"Satan herself. That… is Kerris Jones."

I watched while Kerris Jones's eyes darted from table to table until they came to a stop on us. They narrowed to mere slits before she began moving in our direction. She was a big woman. Not just overweight but overall big. She had to be at least six feet tall. Her bottle-blonde hair was cut in a sharp bob, the dead straight strands barely moving.

"Doris!" Kerris boomed, voice unnecessarily loud considering she was only a few feet from our table.

Doris glanced up as if she didn't know Kerris had arrived. "Oh, hi, Kerris." Digging in her purse, she pulled out a compact and a tube of lipstick and proceeded to touch up her makeup.

"You look nice. Who dressed you? Drag Queens 'R Us?" Kerris inquired sweetly.

"You look lovely, Kerris. I'm so sorry I couldn't attend your funeral last year," Doris shot back without missing a beat. I leaned back in my chair and watched the exchange unfolding in front of me. I could see what Doris had meant about Kerris. She was the type of person who would steamroll you, quite literally, into doing whatever she wanted.

"You missed the meeting today," Kerris said. "Three strikes, and you're out."

Doris arched a brow. "Oh? Another new rule? Actually, I was there. I had to leave early. Another appointment to attend."

Kerris stiffened. "What could possibly have been so important you had to leave?"

Even I bristled at that. Kerris clearly took her role as mayor very seriously, which meant knowing everyone's business. I was eager to hear Doris's response. She didn't disappoint.

"I had to have my hemorrhoids lanced."

Kerris blanched, her hand clutching her pearls.

"Do you want to see?" Doris offered, starting to stand, her hands going to the button on her pants. "You know, as proof for the Committee minutes?"

Kerris waved her back into her seat. "That won't be necessary." She turned her attention to me. "And you must be poor old John's long-lost niece. I'm Mayor Jones. It is my honor to welcome you to Gravestone."

I inclined my head slightly. "Great niece," I automatically corrected. "And thank you."

"Will you be staying long?" she asked.

"Depends."

"On?"

"Lots of things."

Her nostrils flared, belying her irritation at my deliberately vague answers. I'd come across people like her before. She was nothing but a bully, using her size and her position to intimidate and threaten people into getting her own way.

"Well," she huffed, pulling herself up even taller. "Maybe you'd consider dropping by my office where we can have more of a chat?"

"Why would I want to do that?" I asked, truly curious at such an invitation.

Kerris blinked, unused to having her invitations

questioned. "So we can discuss how we may be able to help each other, my dear."

"With what?"

Doris snickered, and I had to bite the inside of my cheek to keep from smiling.

"Your great uncle's house, for one," she snapped, annoyance rolling off her in waves. A sheen of sweat covered her face, and beneath the heavy layer of foundation, a hint of red peeked through. "It's unsafe. Council will be issuing a notice to have it demolished."

I nodded my head, not surprised by the sudden turn the conversation had taken. "Is that right? So, you have a detailed surveyor's report stating that the property is unstable? Because, from what I understand, John Smith was a carpenter of good standing in this town, and he built that house himself, which would lead me to believe he built it good and strong."

I pushed back my chair and stood. At five foot six, it didn't bring us to eye level exactly, but she was no longer towering over me while I was seated. "Furthermore," I continued, "even if the house is demolished, I still own the land, and who knows? Maybe I'll approach my neighbors to buy their land, and I'll expand and build a big old mansion on the mangroves. Which reminds me—maybe I will drop in after all to peruse the boardwalk plans. You know the ones? Just because John Smith is dead doesn't mean the fight is over."

"What?" she exclaimed, the color draining from her face before returning in a tidal wave of red. Her mouth opened and closed like a fish gasping for breath before she swiveled on her heel and stormed out, the floor protesting in loud creaks beneath her heavy footfalls.

"Oh, my God, that was gold!" Doris cackled. "But a word to the wise. Watch your back. You've just made an enemy of the mayor. She's about to make your life hell."

At precisely one minute and twenty-nine seconds past midnight, Doris pulled up outside my house, the Impala idling, headlights out.

"Why the subterfuge?" I asked, sliding into the passenger seat. Doris was dressed all in black. Black pants, a black blouse buttoned up to her chin—she even had a black beanie pulled over her silver locks. She had to be hot in the cat burglar outfit, and I don't mean hot as in phwoar. I mean hot as in temperature.

"I don't want anyone to see us," she whispered.

"You don't think your red car might stand out?"

"Not in the dark." She pulled away from the curb at a reasonably sedate pace.

"You can turn the headlights on, Doris," I said, keeping a firm hold of the door. "Please."

"But—"

"You'll attract more attention driving with the lights off," I pointed out, sensing she was about to argue the point. Doris shot me a look that was impossible to decipher in the darkness of the cab. "You're good at this."

"What, sneaking around in the middle of the night?" I scoffed. "I was a teenager too. Once."

"You snuck out a lot?" Doris asked, flicking the headlights on to my eternal relief.

"You could say that." The truth was, I snuck out constantly. My foster home journey hadn't been smooth. My last home, from sixteen to when I turned eighteen and was finally in charge of my own life, I'd snuck out most nights to keep out of the clutches of my handsy, totally inappropriate foster father. Even the memory of it, so many years later, was enough to make my skin crawl.

Keen to divert attention away from myself, I blurted, "Tell me about John Smith."

"Hmm. Let me see. He was a bit of a grumpy, cantankerous old man, but he wouldn't hurt a fly. He was an excellent carpenter, yet incredibly humble. He did not like to be the center of attention. Probably why he built his house out on Berryman Street. Most everyone else in town is vying for a sea view, but not John. He wanted peace and quiet and privacy."

"Why do you think he killed himself?" I was curious why no one had brought up my fictitious uncle's suicide. If Deputy Biden hadn't spilled the beans, I would never have known.

"I don't think he did," Doris said.

I turned to face her, her features lit by the dashboard lights. "You don't? How come?"

"That man had nothing to die for. He had absolutely no reason to take his own life. He was in reasonable shape health-wise for a man in his seventies. He was not in financial difficulties. He was a loner, he'd always enjoyed his own company, so I don't believe he was lonely either."

"What do you think happened?"

"I think someone staged it to look that way." She shot me a look out of the corner of her eye before turning her attention back to the road. "But I'm thinking you already know that."

"Like I said, I didn't know the man. He's a total stranger to me, so I couldn't say one way or another if he was in a fragile state of mind." But she was right. As soon as the deputy had told me he'd taken his own life, I'd struggled to believe that was the truth. And what of Steve, the stranger who'd come calling, expecting some sort of rendezvous with John on Friday? What did that mean, if anything?

"Do you think he'd climb up into that tree, tie a rope around his neck, and swan dive off?" Doris asked.

"I would have said no until I saw the way you climbed that tree today."

She snorted. "Pilates. Of which John Smith did not partake. He was reasonably healthy, yes, but I doubt very much he was capable of climbing a tree. Not with that bum knee of his."

"Is that what they say happened? That he climbed the tree and then jumped off a branch?"

"Yup, and I agree. It's a farfetched tale if ever I heard one. Far easier and much less strenuous to simply loop the rope over a branch, climb a ladder and then kick the ladder away."

Doris had clearly given this some thought. "I'm guessing there was no ladder?" I asked.

"Nope. And the funny thing? John's ladder was missing. Still is. Usually keeps it tied to the back of his truck."

"On that metal frame thing?"

Doris nodded. "He used that to carry wood, drywall, that type of thing. And he always had his ladder up there. Even when he wasn't working a job."

I mulled over what she'd said while Doris lapsed into silence, thankfully remaining focused on driving. Rather than her usual breakneck speeds, she crawled along at a snail's pace, but I knew better than to complain. I think I actually preferred the snail's pace version.

Eventually, we reached the road out of town. Doris slowed to a stop, the engine idling.

"This is it," she said.

I peered out the side window. "No, it's not. Pretty sure the workmen said it was at least one mile in and marked with a tree shaped like a Y."

"I meant it metaphorically," Doris said, slamming her foot down on the accelerator and planting it. The

Impala fishtailed, the rear tires unable to find purchase on the gravel surface of the road.

"Doris!" I shrieked, hands slapping on the dash to stabilize myself. "Take it easy. What happened to stealth mode?"

"Oh, shoot, sorry, I forgot!" She immediately eased her foot off the throttle, and we proceeded down the road at a much more sedate, but still too fast, pace. The Impala managed to find every single pothole, and one particularly nasty crater had my head slamming into the roof of the car.

"Ouch!" I rubbed my head and glared at Doris. "Have you considered avoiding the potholes?" I grumbled.

"What's that, dear?" She cupped a hand to her ear as if she hadn't heard me when I knew darn well she had. Her smirk gave her away.

"Slow down!" I pointed at the tree up ahead, caught in the headlights. "I think that's it."

The Impala rolled to a stop. Sure enough, there was a tree shaped like a Y. The weeds around the base had been trampled, probably from where the workmen had explored. They'd said there was a hidden road, and I squinted at the dead bushes to the right of the tree.

"They look staged to you?" I asked but didn't wait for an answer. Opening the door, I hopped out of the car and made my way across the recently graded portion of the road, over the mound of dirt that had been pushed up the side from the grader to the tree.

Using the trunk as balance, I maneuvered around to the dead bushes. I could just make out boot prints.

"This has to be it," I said under my breath. Reaching out, I grabbed hold of one of the bushes with both hands and pulled. To my surprise, it pulled right out of the ground, and I staggered back, nearly landing on my butt. Tossing the bush to the side, I went back for another and another. Within thirty seconds, I'd thrown them all to one side, and sure enough, there was an overgrown track.

"A hidden road," I said, then remembered Doris was still in the car. I turned to give her the thumbs up when I heard the revving of the Impala and the sudden swing of headlights alerting me that Doris was done waiting. The vehicle shot backward, there was a crunch and a grind as she changed gears, and that's when I realized she fully intended to drive the Impala down the secret track we'd just discovered. Only one problem. The bank of dirt piled up alongside the road. If the Impala had four-wheel drive, we might be able to do it if the vehicle were high enough. But the Impala? There was no way she'd have the clearance.

"No, Doris, wait!" I cupped my hands around my mouth to be heard over the roar of the engine, but either she couldn't hear me, or she chose to ignore me, for the Impala shot forward, heading straight for me. There was an odd crunching noise and a puff of dust as the front wheels mounted the bank of dirt in an upward trajectory and then stayed there as the vehicle bottomed out. Doris's solution was to press her foot harder on the accelerator, which only resulted in the back tires spinning harder and gravel shooting out behind the car.

"Stop!" I yelled. She finally listened, eased her foot off the accelerator, and leaned out the driver's window.

"Am I stuck?" she asked.

I rolled my eyes. "Yes." She was stuck and stuck fast. Nothing but a tow truck would get the Impala out of its current predicament.

Doris turned off the engine and climbed out, surveying her car. "Well, shoot," she said, hands on hips.

"I don't think you bent the axle," I said. "The dirt is soft, recently graded. Unless, of course, you hit a rock under all that."

Doris patted the hood of the Impala. "You'll be right, girl; we'll get you out. After we've explored this track." She walked around the back of the car to the passenger side, reached into the glove compartment, and pulled out a flashlight before returning to the driver's side, turning off the headlights, and removing the keys from the ignition.

"Isn't it dangerous, leaving it in the dark like that? Shouldn't you put your hazards on?"

"Good idea." Next thing, the darkness of the night was lit up with the orange flicker of the indicators as they blinked off and on. "We'd better get moving. While we don't get a lot of traffic along this road at this time of night, Calder has been doing extra patrols due to the state of the road."

All the more reason to move fast. "Let's go," I said,

waiting for her to scramble over the dirt verge and join me, the beam of the flashlight swinging wildly.

"What do you think is out here?" Doris asked as we made our way past the pile of dead shrubs, following the track that had been carved out. The two ruts indicated whoever had been out here had been driving, but the level of weed and grass encroachment said they hadn't been here in quite some time.

"You probably have a better idea than I do." My walking boot thumped as we walked, and I knew I'd pay for this later. As it was, I'd dosed myself with painkillers before leaving home. "Is there a drug problem in Gravestone?"

"There's a high trade in arthritis meds," Doris said.

Not exactly what I was thinking. In my experience, a hidden road tended to mean that whatever was at the end was something no one wanted found. My last secret road had taken me to an underground operation selling fairy dust. Dozens of fairies had been captured and held captive, a coven of witches harvesting their magic dust and selling it on the black market. It didn't sound so terrible, but stealing the fairy dust left the fairies permanently injured, unable to fly. And without being able to fly? They tended to die shortly after. All in all, a horrible situation.

"I had an interesting visitor last night," I said, my mind circling back to John and the circumstances of his death.

"Oh?" Doris easily kept pace by my side; she wasn't even winded, whereas I seemed to be puffing rather heavily. So much for being an elite agent. Out of action for a few days and already unfit. As soon as this walking boot was off, I'd have to hit the training circuit hard.

"Yeah, some guy named Steve. Didn't seem to understand that John was dead. Wanted to know if the thing was still on for Friday night."

"What thing?"

"Exactly. He wouldn't say. He was very cagey. When I told him who I was, he said John had spoken of me."

Doris guffawed. "That's rich. John didn't know you even existed." She stopped walking and looked at me in the moonlight. "Did he?"

I shrugged. "Not as far as I know. Like I said, he and my mom were estranged. They hadn't spoken in years —longer than my lifetime." I wondered if I'd ever feel guilty about the number of lies that flowed off my tongue. Then I wondered why I was even wondering such a thing. Telling lies to protect my undercover status had been part of my life for so long it was second nature, and I never questioned it. Until now. A scant thirty-six hours into my stay at Gravestone, I was not only losing my touch but also questioning myself on the ethics of lying.

We continued walking, lost in our own thoughts. Mine had drifted from John to Seth Saltzman. Assuming the bones were Seth's, were their deaths related? And if John's death was suspicious, as Doris suggested, why had the police ruled it a suicide?

"Was Seth ever reported missing?" I asked.

"Not by anyone in Gravestone. I think there's an arrest warrant out for him because he failed to show for the court hearing into the fraud charge."

"For his so-called cancer?"

"Yeah. The townsfolk put together a class action, and he was scheduled to appear before the magistrate in Corpus Christi. Only he never showed. And that automatically earned him an arrest warrant."

"And no one's seen him since." But the guy may have done a runner, gone into hiding. America was a big country. He could be lying low anywhere. If it were me, I'd sure as heck get my butt out of Texas at the very least.

Doris grabbed my arm in a steely grip, dragging me to a halt. "There!" She pointed with the flashlight, and through the shadows and the trees, I could just make out a wooden structure. It was situated off the makeshift road, but a rough path led to it.

"Is it a barn?" I asked, taking in the weathered boards.

"Could be." A cloud passed over the moon. The only light was Doris's flashlight that trembled ever so slightly as she pointed it at the barn.

"Are you scared?" I teased.

"Of a spooky old barn in the middle of nowhere?" she asked. "Hardly." She stomped toward the barn as if to prove her point. I followed, my boot thumping on the ground. The air was still, the hum of insects and the odd screech from a night bird—most likely an owl— were the only noises aside from our less than stealthy approach. Humidity hung over us like a hot, wet blanket, and despite the lack of sun, I was soaked with sweat.

We reached the door to find it locked with a chain and padlock. Doris tugged at it. "Locked."

"You have a hair clip?" I asked.

Doris pointed to the beanie covering her white locks. "Do I look like I have a hair clip?"

I shrugged. "You seem the kind of person who is always prepared."

She slid her fingers under one side of the beanie, wriggled them around, then triumphantly held out a hair clip. "Ta da."

I couldn't help but laugh. "Thanks." Taking it from her, I pried the clip apart, then slid it into the lock. Two seconds and the padlock clicked open.

"Neat. Learn that in a book too?" Doris asked.

Darn, I'd totally forgotten that the average person did not know how to pick locks. "Of course." Yet another lie. They were stacking up. If the day ever came when I'd be forced to face up to the mountain of lies I'd told in my lifetime, I'd be doomed.

Doris sniffed. "Well. It's not rocket surgery."

I chuckled, unhooked the chain, and pulled the door open, stepping back to let Doris precede me. I followed closely behind. As soon as the door opened, I'd felt the change in the air, and a shiver danced up my spine, making the hairs on the back of my neck stand on end. I looked back over my shoulder. Nothing but darkness, the moon peeking out behind the clouds every now and then, obscuring what little light there was.

"Holy sh—" Doris began, her flashlight trained in the middle of the barn.

I followed the beam of light and saw what she'd seen. A body sprawled on the floor. A long since dead body, more a skeleton wearing clothes.

I nudged Doris. "Move closer. Is the left arm missing?"

We skirted closer, the flashlight bobbing with our movements. The beam of light hit the shoulders and trailed down one arm. The other arm? Missing, from the elbow down.

"Eureka," I whispered. We'd found the rest of the body.

Pulling out my phone, I was about to dial when I realized the only number I had on my phone was Doris's. "What's the sheriff's number?" I asked her.

"Huh?" She seemed in a daze, her eyes glued to the skeleton on the floor.

"We have to call the sheriff," I said, placing a comforting hand on her shoulder.

"Do we, though?"

Her answer shocked me. "Doris! Yes. We do. We've just discovered the remains of who we assume is Seth Saltzman. There comes a time when we do, in fact, have to call in the authorities." And I needed to stay out of it, for if the sheriff dug too hard, he'd discover my true identity, and that meant not only trouble for me, but for Gravestone too.

I crouched next to the bones, searching for anything that would tell me the cause of death. The plaid shirt had no tares or rips, no bullet holes or blood stains. What remained of his left arm was tucked close to his side, but his right arm was outstretched, the fingers curled into a fist.

"Look." Doris unfurled the fingers, revealing a black stone with a rune drawn on it. "This is magic."

My eyes bugged out on stalks. "What do you know of magic?" I blurted, rattled that she'd even mention such a thing.

Doris drew her gaze from the rune to me, raising the flashlight to shine it in my face.

"Hey!" I protested, bringing an arm up to shield my eyes. "Quit it."

"I know what you are, Holly Day," she declared. "You're a witch."

Her words echoed around the barn, and I stared at her, shocked to the core. How could she know? Unless…

"Doris Shutt," I shot back. "Are *you* a witch?" It would explain so much, like her insane strength and agility. She was using magic, but she hid it well. I hadn't detected it at all.

We engaged in a staring match, neither prepared to back down despite my eyeballs being on fire and drying out. Eventually, Doris blinked and said, "Takes one to know one."

CHAPTER

Twelve

"This has to stay between us," I said. "I'm serious, Doris."

"You think I don't know that?" Doris popped a hip and rested her hand on it. "Who are you with? SIA? Council? Bounty?"

Seemed there was more to Doris Shutt than met the eye. I had two choices. Tell Doris the truth and hope she could keep her mouth shut and not blow my cover. Or silence her. Permanently. Lucky for Doris, I quite liked her.

"SIA," I said. "And you?" She had to be, to recognize one of her own.

"SIA. Retired."

My eyes narrowed. "Did Scott Harding send you here?" If Scott was responsible, that just might explain her name.

"Nope." She turned her flashlight back to the body. "But we have a problem."

One dead body. Death by magic? Or death by human hand?

"What does the rune mean, do you know?" I asked. "Is it a hex?"

"I think so, but it's hard to see. Take a photo of it, would you?"

"Good idea." After snapping some close-ups of the rune, I took photos of the crime scene, knowing that it would be off-limits as soon as the sheriff was notified. "Are there any other witches in Gravestone?" I asked as I worked, my mind immediately going to the women's committee. Were they a secret coven?

Doris shrugged. "Some. Gravestone is the ideal place for supernaturals to hide out. It's on a ley line that keeps our powers hidden."

Interesting. No wonder Harding had sent me here. A ley line that hid supernaturals was the perfect spot, and I wondered how many others he stashed here. Quite a few, I'd imagine. I'd question Doris on this whole thing later. Right now, we had a more pressing problem. "I'm assuming the sheriff isn't of a supernatural variety?"

"He's as human as they come," Doris confirmed, hustling away to begin searching the rest of the barn. I joined her. We needed something, a clue as to who had done this. There was no way Seth's death had been natural causes. He was murdered. The why was obvious. Given that the barn was empty save for a couple of boxes that practically disintegrated at a touch, it didn't take us long to come up empty-handed.

"Now what?" Doris asked.

"We call the sheriff."

"Cover story?" Doris asked, pulling her phone from her bra.

"The truth—as close to it without giving us away. Tell him we overheard the workers talking about a hidden track and decided to check it out. He was going to find out anyway, considering your car is stuck out on the main road."

While Doris made the call, I circled the remains, studying them. I really wanted to roll the victim onto his back but knew Calder would have a heart attack if we touched the body. Plus, we didn't need any of our DNA to contaminate the scene. Calder already suspected I was involved. I didn't need to add fuel to that particular fire.

I straightened from where I'd been examining the floor. "What confuses me is why hide the body out here? Why not bury it? Instead, they've left him somewhat exposed."

Doris chewed her lip, messing up her lipstick. "You're right. It's a horrible hiding place. While the barn is remote and kinda hidden, anyone could accidentally stumble across it."

"Unless that's what they wanted? Someone was counting on his body being found?"

"They've had a long wait," Doris mumbled, standing at who we assumed to be Seth's feet, her eyes trailing along his body.

I turned my attention to the rune in his hand. Magic. It had to be. But why did Seth have the rune? Was it a form of protection, in which case, it failed? Or had the killer used it as a weapon?

"What you said before? About Gravestone being on a ley line and hiding our magic… does that mean I can use my magic, and it won't be detected?" Harding had told me under no circumstances was I to use my magic. Had he lied? *The irony!*

"Pretty much." She shrugged.

"The Gravestone Women's Committee… are they a coven?"

She grinned. "Not exactly. The sheriff will be here any minute; we can discuss all that later. Right now, we need to find out who is responsible for this." She jerked her thumb toward Seth.

"And how did his hand end up at my house?"

"Exactly."

"If this is Seth," I jerked my head toward the body dressed in faded blue jeans and a plaid shirt, size eleven scuffed and worn boots, "was he killed by magic? And was he a witch or warlock or some other supernatural entity?"

"You want to know if we're dealing with a standard human homicide or if this is paranormal." Doris crossed her arms, eyes locked on Seth as if she could find the answers in his bones.

"He decomposed quickly," I observed, although I already knew the heat and humidity of Gravestone contributed to that.

"The heat. And the critters."

"But the body doesn't look disturbed. If animals got

to him, his bones would be strewn around." The body was remarkably intact except for the left forearm and hand, which was currently wrapped in plastic and duct-taped to a branch on the cedar elm in my backyard.

"Insect critters," she clarified.

The sound of our names being called carried on the night air. The sheriff had arrived. Exchanging a look with Doris, I stepped out of the barn, cupped my hands around my mouth, and yelled back, "Here!"

I could see a light in the distance, watched as Calder jogged along the dirt track, the light bobbing up and down, casting arcs in the inky blackness of the night sky. He appeared out of the darkness; his powerful flashlight swung over the barn, then landed on me, where I stood in the open doorway.

"You okay?" He slowed to a brisk walk.

"We're fine."

"Do I even want to know what the two of you are doing out here? And how on earth did Doris's car end up halfway up the bank?"

"Sheer curiosity, I'm afraid," I replied. "We overheard some workmen talking about a hidden road they'd discovered, and well, basically, we wanted to beat them to the punch. They said they were going to check it out when they'd finished sealing the road."

Calder's brow furrowed. "Why? It's just a road. Not even. More of a track. A path."

"But it was *hidden*." And I, for one, could not resist a mystery. If the track hadn't been deliberately hidden, I wouldn't have been interested. But it had been, so I was. It was one of the reasons I'd become an SIA agent to begin with. I loved a good puzzle, and I was tenacious. Not everyone thought those traits endearing.

"Oh, good, you're here." Doris stepped out of the barn. "We found Seth. What's left of him."

Calder brushed past me, muttering something under his breath I couldn't make out. Pretty sure it was about Doris and me poking our noses in where they didn't belong.

Shrugging, I followed. He stood next to Doris, the pair of them staring at the skeleton on the floor of the barn.

"Weird, huh?" Doris quipped, crossing her arms.

"You got that right. What is this, occult?" Calder pointed to the rune.

Doris rammed her elbow into his ribs so hard he staggered back. "It's Seth Saltzman, isn't it? I'm right, aren't I?" She threw me a wink over her shoulder.

"The clothing would be something Seth would wear, but we'll have to wait for forensics to confirm." Calder walked around the body, snapping photos with his phone. "May have a wallet or other ID in his pocket." He crouched by the remains and carefully patted down the skeleton, extracting a wallet from the front pocket of the jeans. Flipping it open, he examined the contents.

"Well?" Doris demanded.

"Seth Saltzman," Calder confirmed, closing the wallet. Reaching into his back pocket, he pulled out a Ziplock bag and dropped the wallet into it. Then he picked up the rune, holding it up while Doris shone the flashlight on it. "What's this?"

Now that I could get a good look at the rune, I was shocked. My hand went to the similar rune inked onto my collarbone.

"See that?" I whispered to Doris.

"See what? The rock?" she whispered back.

"No. The rune carved into the rock."

"Kinda looks like yours, right?"

Of course, our whispering drew Calder's attention. "What are you two whispering about? Do you know something about this?" He waved the rock in the air.

I automatically shook my head. "Nope. Just wondering what Seth was doing with a rock in his hand. Kinda odd, don't you think?"

Calder's eyes narrowed, and his jaw hardened. "I think you know more than you're saying."

I blinked, not sure what to say to that, so I said nothing. He pointed at my face. "That right there? That gives you away."

I reeled back in shock. "What? My face?" I turned to Doris. "What's wrong with my face?"

Doris rounded on Calder. "Yeah, what's wrong with her face? That's just plain rude, Calder. I expected better from you."

His face suffused with color, and a vein pulsed in his temple. "That wasn't what I meant, and you know it." He pointed to the barn door. "Out. Both of you, wait outside."

And that's when the unthinkable happened. Doris

turned right, I turned left, and we collided in the middle, which wouldn't have been a big deal, except thanks to the walking boot, I lost my balance and staggered, bumping into Calder. The rune was jostled from his grip, and I automatically stuck my hand out to catch it. As soon as the rock touched my palm, I may as well have been dipped in a vat of acid. The pain was immediate and excruciating.

It felt like my body was being slashed with thousands of razors, my magic draining away with each cut. Pain radiated through me, from the top of my head to the tips of my toes. A scream echoed in my head, and tears streamed down my cheeks before I felt an arm wrap around my waist and swing me off my feet, the rune slipping through my fingers to fall to the floor.

CHAPTER
Thirteen

"My eyeballs are on fire, my muscles are trying to peel themselves away from the bone, and my skin is made of acid. Other than that, I feel great."

Doris beamed. "Excellent. No harm done then."

I rolled my eyes, then immediately regretted it. I hadn't been lying when I said they were on fire. Doris had hustled me out of the barn, convincing Calder to tow her car off the bank so she could get me home to my allergy meds. As far as excuses went, it was flimsy. Still, he'd obliged, torn between wanting to get me the medical assistance I so clearly required and needing to stay at the crime scene.

"Here. Drink this. It'll help." Doris held out a cup. As I struggled to sit up from my position on the camp bed in my living room, she placed the cup on the floor by the side of the bed, then grabbed me under the arms and heaved me into a sitting position.

"Thanks," I wheezed, my energy depleted.

"Drink." She shoved the steaming cup into my hand, and I automatically took a sip.

"Yikes!" I gasped. "What is this? Gasoline?"

"Stop being so dramatic." Doris waved a hand, indicating to keep drinking. "It's a little something to remove the toxins from your system. That was some bad juju, huh?"

I nodded. "The worst. I've never come across anything like it before."

"I'm thinking this might tell us something." She held up the black rune Calder had found in Seth's hand. The same rune that had dipped me in acid.

"Doris! Did you steal that?"

She shrugged. "I borrowed it. We both know the cops won't know what to make of it, and it'll sit in an evidence bag gathering dust. Well, not exactly gathering dust since it'll be inside a plastic bag, but you know what I mean."

"I'm surprised Calder didn't notice you swipe it." I took another sip of gasoline, grimacing as my insides continued to burn and simultaneously melt.

"He was too busy carrying you." She shrugged.

"How can you even bear to touch it? Man, it zapped me with a million volts of electricity."

She tossed the rune up and down in her hand. "I think this is what killed Seth. That it was charged with something lethal. And you got the remaining dose. Not enough to kill, but enough to give you a nasty zap. Now? Now it's nothing but a rock."

"But… Calder handled it before I did. Why didn't it affect him?"

"Maybe it only affects people who have magic pumping through their veins?"

"So, Seth Saltzman was a witch?"

Doris shrugged. "Not that I was aware of."

My head started to thump just thinking about it.

"How did you get your car out of the ditch?" I asked, changing the subject.

"It wasn't in a ditch. It was on a bank."

"Whatever." Another sip of gasoline. Lordy, but I better not burp lest the flames that would surely shoot from my mouth would set the house on fire.

"I convinced Calder to tow it off the mound of dirt. He wanted to call an ambulance, but I talked him down, said that it'd be faster if I took you since it was one in the morning, and the volunteer ambulance crew would be asleep."

"Let me see the rune." I held out my hand, and Doris placed the stone in my palm. I held my breath, waiting for a surge of pain, but nothing happened. "This looks similar to my birthmark." Doris snorted, and I looked at her. "What?"

"That's not a birthmark. It's a mark, all right, but you weren't born with it. It's a protection spell." I remembered she'd said the same thing before when she and Calder had first seen the mark on my collarbone.

It was my turn to snort. "Well, it didn't do a very good job tonight!"

"Actually, I think it did exactly what it was meant to do. Otherwise, you'd be dead."

I sobered. "Really? You think the magic was that powerful?"

"I'm thinking Seth is an ordinary human who was targeted as a sacrifice. This rune was hexed to kill him. You discharged the remainder of the hex—because you *are* a witch."

I frowned. "I'm not following."

"Okay, think of it like this. Whoever did this created this rune," she took it from me and held it up, "to target Seth. The hex will only kick in when Seth holds the stone. Any other human touches it, and nada, zip, zilch. But should another witch touch it? Zap. You're toast. That's the thing with hexes. They can be quite specific." She tossed the rune in the air and caught it. "You didn't get the full dose because part of the magic had already been discharged, killing Seth. You got the tail end."

"Let me tell you, the tail end had quite a kick." Flynn, who'd been sitting at the end of the bed with concern in his eyes, chose that moment to run up my leg, making himself comfortable on my lap. I stroked a hand over his fur. "It's okay," I assured him. "I'm fine." Placing the cup of gasoline on the floor, I lay back down. My head was swimming. I felt like I was going to hurl.

"Runes are usually protection talismans," Doris said. "I've never seen one used as a hex before."

"I wish I had my grimoire." I sighed. Harding had

forbidden me from bringing anything that could identify me as a witch. Instead, my bulging grimoire, chock full of useful information on magic and witchcraft that I'd collected through the years, was locked in a safe at SIA headquarters.

"Oh, shit," I whispered, a horrible thought filtering into my mind.

"Well, don't do it here; get up and use the bathroom," Doris grumbled. She'd settled into the camp chair, her chin slowly descending to rest on her chest as she dozed off.

"No. Not literally." I was having trouble thinking, my mind a thick fog. What was in that gasoline? Or was it the residual magic I'd dipped myself into that was making coherent thought impossible? "If there really is a mole at the SIA," I mumbled, "they could have access to my grimoire. That book holds a lot of secrets."

"Does your boss know that?" Doris slurred back. "What was his name again? Hardly?"

"Harding. And no. No one knows what's in my grimoire except me."

My eyelids were so heavy I couldn't keep them open anymore. As they fluttered closed, I heard the faint rumble of thunder in the distance, and my last coherent thought was that I hoped the roof didn't leak.

I awoke to Flynn draped across my forehead, rain on the roof, and the smell of coffee in the air. Scooping up the rat, I sat up and settled him on my pillow. He promptly turned his back and curled into a ball, apparently content to keep on sleeping, his fur now indigo blue.

After hustling upstairs to use the bathroom, splashing some water on my face, and changing clothes, I thumped back downstairs, casting a glance out the window at the stormy day outside. My watch said it was six in the morning. Funny, it felt like I'd slept longer, but it seemed a few short hours got the job done.

The coffee pot was on in the kitchen, with a note propped up against it.

"*Call me when you wake up. Doris.*" Pouring myself a cup, I took a sip before dialing the only number on my phone.

Doris answered on the first ring. "You're finally awake."

"What do you mean finally? It's only six, still early."

"Early?" She guffawed. "Hun, it's six in the evening."

I almost spit out my coffee. "What?" It couldn't be! I turned my eyes toward the kitchen window and the gloomy day outside. Sure, I guessed the heavy rain clouds could equally belong to dusk as to dawn.

"Girl, you've been asleep for near on sixteen hours."

I blinked in shock. I mean, I must have needed it, obviously, but holy heck, I'd lost an entire day.

"How are you feeling?" Doris asked.

"Actually, I feel pretty good." It was true. The aftereffects of the hex and the gasoline drink had gone. The enforced rest had done my foot some good as well; it felt remarkably better.

"What did I miss?" I asked, leaning against the kitchen counter and sipping my coffee.

"So, the bills are washed, the laundry is paid, the clothes are in the oven, and the last load of dinner is in the dryer."

"Doris, did *you* get any sleep?" The last thing I remembered, she was dozing in my camp chair.

"A little. Calder has been by your house three times."

"He has? Did he knock?" I hadn't heard a thing. Surely, I'd have woken up if he'd knocked.

"Oh, he knocked. Pounded even. Dragged me over to go in and check on you."

Wow. I didn't recall any of it.

"I told him it was just your allergy meds, and I'd get you to call him when you woke up. Which I guess you should do."

"What does he want, do you know?"

"Something about a statement from last night."

"Have you given one?"

"Of course. He says it wasn't very helpful. He says my mind wanders like an inebriated squirrel, and I lack the ability to…" She trailed off.

"To what?" I bit my lip to keep from giggling. Calder had Doris pegged.

"To recall detail and remain focused is what I think

he said, but to be honest, I wasn't really paying attention." Case in point.

"Fine. I'll call. What's his number?"

"He left a business card on your door. Well, good luck. I'm off to watch Wheel of Fortune." She hung up before I could respond. With a shrug, I set my coffee down and hobbled to the front door. Sure enough, a crisp white business card was tucked in the screen door. Plucking it free, I read the words 'call me,' scrawled on the back in blue ink. The front of the card had the Texas police logo and Sheriff Joshua Calder's name, e-mail, and phone number.

Retreating to the kitchen, I dialed.

"Calder." He answered on the second ring.

"This is Holly Day." I screwed up my nose, hating my fake name.

"Thank you for calling," he replied, sounding one hundred percent professional. "I was concerned for your welfare."

"So I hear. I'm fine. Nasty allergic reaction," I lied. "And my allergy medication knocks me out."

"What are you allergic to?"

It wasn't an unreasonable question. "Some organic molecules and biological compounds," I replied, the lie rolling off my tongue without a second thought. "I assume there was something on that rock that didn't agree with me."

"You had a pretty severe reaction. Are you sure you're okay? Doris insisted you didn't need to go to the hospital."

"I'm one hundred percent fine. Doris was right. I just needed my meds and a decent sleep." Time to change the subject. "Have you been able to get a positive ID on the body?" Despite finding Seth's wallet at the scene, I knew Calder would follow up with DNA.

"It's Seth Saltzman," he confirmed.

"Cause of death?"

"Undetermined. And if you don't mind, I'm the one asking questions."

Shoot. "Fire away."

There wasn't much I could tell him that Doris hadn't already supplied.

"I'm not buying that you two decided to go on a late-night drive, on a road under repair, on a *whim*." His voice wasn't exactly a growl, but there was a note of something extra in it, beyond annoyance. He knew we were up to something, and I had a feeling he'd keep digging until he found out what.

"I really don't know what else to tell you, Calder," I offered in the way of placation. "It's the truth. I overheard the workmen talking in River's about the hidden track they'd discovered and was curious."

"What I don't understand is why you felt the need to explore after midnight."

"You'll have to ask Doris that. The timing was on her since I don't have wheels yet."

"Between the two of you…" He trailed off.

"Yes?" I prompted.

"Never mind." His sigh was loud through the phone. "You're okay now?" His voice had changed from that slightly annoyed, aggrieved deep rumble to an even lower baritone, almost like he cared.

"I'm fine. Sorry if I gave you a scare."

"Yes. Well." He cleared his throat, his voice leveling out. "Have a good evening, Holly. Do me a favor? No midnight drives with Doris tonight."

"I have no intention of leaving the house this evening," I assured him. "I have some baking to do."

"You bake?" The way his voice went up three octaves indicated his utter surprise that I partook in such domestic duties.

"Indeed I do," I replied, injecting extra pep into my voice. "Take care, Calder." I disconnected the call before he could respond. Flynn, who'd been asleep on my pillow, darted into the kitchen, onto a chair, then the countertop.

"You heard me say baking, didn't you?" He rubbed a paw over his whiskers as if it was purely coincidental that he was in the kitchen right when I decided to bake.

Thunder rumbled outside, and a flash of lightning lit up the back garden, the cedar elm tree casting ghoulish shadows across the ground. After finishing my coffee, I rinsed the cup and left it to drain on the sink. "So, what'll it be, Flynn? Snickerdoodle's, fudge, or apple fritters?"

Flynn squeaked at all three suggestions, and I raised a brow. "All three, you say? Hmm. You know... why not? Nothing else to do tonight." I was still coming to terms with the fact that it was early evening and not early morning.

An hour later, I was elbow deep in flour when there was a knock at the front door. I glanced at Flynn, licking a mixing spoon, ignoring the summons. "I'll get it, shall I?" I drawled, wiping my hands on a tea towel. Thunder still rumbled, but now it was accompanied by rain, a steady downpour that hadn't eased up in over twenty minutes.

Opening the front door, I was taken aback to see Casey standing there, rain dripping from his coat, the collar turned up. "Casey! Come in. Some weather we're having." I ushered him inside.

"Sorry to interrupt." He flashed those pearly whites while taking off his hat and unzipping his coat. "Figured I should check on you."

My brows shot into my hairline. Had he heard what had happened out at the old barn? "Really?"

But Casey wasn't looking at me. His eyes were on the ceiling. "Yeah. We haven't had rain like this in ages, and to be honest with you, I'm not sure old John's roof will hold up to the onslaught."

We stood there in my living room, side-by-side, gazing at the ceiling. Seconds ticked by with neither of us speaking until the timer went off on the oven, jerking me out of the ever-so-fun game of watching to see if the roof would leak.

"You might want to check upstairs, though, cos this is a two-story house, and if water is leaking through the living room ceiling, then I suspect the roof is gone entirely." I shrugged and headed to the kitchen, turning off the timer and sliding the tray of snickerdoodle's onto a wire rack. Casey appeared in the doorway, looking sheepish.

"Mind if I quickly check upstairs?"

"Sure." I waved him away. "Knock yourself out."

Over the rumble of thunder, I could hear the creak and groan as Casey moved about the upper level, then the heavy thud of his boots on the stairs.

"All good." He appeared in the doorway once more. "I've gotta run. Few folks are dealing with leaks and need help tying down tarps."

"Sure. Thanks for dropping by. Here, take a snickerdoodle with you."

He crossed the room with long, loose strides, snatched up two of the cookies, and with a salute, headed back the way he came. I called out a farewell and left him to let himself out when I heard a commotion at the front door.

"Matthew Casey! What on earth are you doing here?" a female voice rang out.

"Could say the same for you, Mayor," Casey shot back. "If you'll excuse me, I'm just leaving. Holly!" he hollered. "You have another visitor."

I appeared in the kitchen doorway to see Kerris Jones standing on my front porch holding a yellow umbrella.

"Kerris," I greeted her, dusting my palms off on my behind. "To what do I owe the pleasure?"

Her back stiffened, and her lips flattened into a thin line. "My constituents address me as Mayor," she said stiffly.

"Good thing I'm not your constituent then. Would you like to come in?" I was curious what had brought the mayor to my door in such foul weather.

"If I must." She stepped over the threshold, accompanied by a clap of thunder and the lights flickering. How apt.

"Snickerdoodle?" I offered, thumping my way into the kitchen, the mayor trailing behind me, sniffing her disapproval.

The kitchen felt smaller with Kerris Jones in it. Not only her size but her demeanor, as if she were standing in a slum and couldn't stand for the filth to touch her. But if she expected me to be intimidated by her behavior, she'd have a long wait. I'd long since stopped caring about what anyone thought of me—let alone where I lived.

Flynn, whose stomach was bulging at the amount of cookie dough he'd consumed, sat and stared at the mayor, whose eyes had locked on him.

"Is that a... *rat?*"

"Yes. This is Flynn." I folded my arms and waited. Didn't have to wait long. Her face suffused with purple, her eyes bulged, and her mouth opened and closed, mimicking a goldfish until she finally found her words.

"This is a health code violation! You cannot keep vermin inside. This is outrageous. I'm having this place condemned!" she screeched. Flynn and I both cringed, not at her words but the pitch of her voice. I was surprised the window didn't crack.

She ranted on for a solid minute, something about calling the exterminator and the sheriff and that I should be ashamed of myself. I ignored her, busying myself with placing the snickerdoodle's into a container.

"Well?" she finally demanded. "What do you have to say for yourself?"

"Firstly," I smiled sweetly, "this is my *home*, and what I choose to do here is no one else's business except my own. Secondly, Flynn is my pet. Just like people keep cats or dogs as pets, I have a rat. Perfectly legal. And thirdly, I repeat, *this is my home*, and you came here unannounced and uninvited to…what? Yell at me over my choice of pet? In which case, I bid you farewell, *Mayor*. Have a nice evening."

If it were possible, her face suffused with even more color, and her mouth did the goldfish thing again.

"May I use your bathroom?" she finally said.

I don't know what I'd been expecting her to say, but it certainly wasn't that.

"What?" Surely, I'd misheard her?

"Sorry to bother you." Her voice was ice cold, her eyes sharp. She'd regained control of her wayward emotions, and the ice queen was back. "I shall take my leave. But if I may use your bathroom beforehand, that would be much appreciated."

"Sure. Top of the stairs."

She stared at me hard, and I stared right back, unflinching. I didn't know what Kerris Jones was doing here this evening or what she hoped to achieve by challenging me to a staring competition, but if she thought she would win, she thought wrong. I was a champion starer.

Eventually, she conceded defeat and spun on her heel without a word. The stairs creaked and groaned in protest as she thumped up them, rage in every step. I heard her try and close the bathroom door and couldn't contain the grin when she realized the door was warped and would not stay closed.

"Well?" I whispered to Flynn, whose fur was actually standing on end. "What do you think that was all about?"

Flynn's paws moved manically, slashing through the air, desperately trying to tell me something. The only problem was I didn't speak sign language. Nor rat.

"What is it?" I hissed. "I don't understand!" We both heard the toilet flush and the faucet run and knew she'd be back downstairs within a few short minutes.

"Look, I'll get rid of her, okay?" I tried to reassure Flynn, running a gentle hand over his fur, which had finally settled, but as the thump, thump, thump of her feet on the stairs boomed through the house, it stood on end again.

I met Kerris at the bottom of the stairs. "Thanks for

dropping by," I said, arm outstretched to indicate the front door. "But I think it's best if you leave."

"Don't you want to know why I stopped by?" she asked haughtily.

"Nope." Obviously a lie. I was burning with curiosity, but I refused to give her the satisfaction of voicing it. "Drive safe now." Opening the front door, I stood aside so she could leave. I was beginning to think she had no intention of leaving when she stayed rooted to the spot. Eventually, she crossed the room and stepped over the threshold.

"I came to present you a beyond generous offer on the house," she said.

"*This* house?" Of course, I knew she meant this house. I was just having way too much fun messing with her.

"Yes," she ground out. "This house."

"As I told you earlier, I'm not selling. Not yet anyway. And if I do decide to sell, I'll be contacting a realtor, no private offers."

"You haven't heard what I'm prepared to pay." She leaned forward and whispered an obscene amount of money in my ear. I was shocked. She was prepared to pay at least three times more than what the house was worth.

She straightened, a smug look on her face, as if thinking that once she told me the offer, I'd be overcome with greed and accept.

"Generous," I conceded, nodding. "But I'm afraid I must decline."

"What?" Her screeching was about to start up again, I could tell, so I shut the door in her face. I was halfway to the kitchen when the knocking started. With irritation dancing across my skin, I flung open the door.

"Listen—" I began, only to pull up when it wasn't Kerris Jones knocking on my door but one of the women who'd helped with the cleaning of the house. "Oh! Sorry, I thought you were someone else."

"Kerris just left." The white-haired woman with the kind brown eyes smiled almost apologetically. "Sorry to bother you…."

"Please, come on in." I held the door open wider, allowing her entry. "Denise, isn't it?" I recalled seeing her cleaning at the police station and she'd been part of the cleaning party who'd descended on my place when I first arrived.

"Yes, Denise Hurt." She smiled, seemingly pleased I'd remember her name.

Denise Hurt. So… another witch? Only I couldn't very well come out and ask her, not when we were meant to be a secret. Doris knew what was what and who was who in this town. I'd have to ask her about Denise next time I spoke with her.

"Snickerdoodle, Denise?" I asked, leading the way to the kitchen. Flynn, who'd hidden behind a bag of flour, poked his head out, afraid it was Kerris back again.

"That would be lovely, thank you," Denise said, taking one of the snickerdoodle's and nibbling on it. Despite telling myself I wouldn't eat any more cookies tonight, I picked one up and took a bite. Mmmm, so soft and chewy.

"What can I help you with, Denise?" I prompted. I wasn't used to having visitors, and three in quick succession was not only a surprise but annoying. I was used to being alone. This revolving door of guests had my shoulders tense and my nerves on edge.

Denise cleared her throat. "This is probably going to sound a little odd," she began. I almost laughed. Ever since arriving in Gravestone, things had been odd. What was one more?

"I'm working on the history of Gravestone, and before he passed, John said he had some books that I could borrow. Only…" She trailed off, fiddling with her snickerdoodle, crumbs dropping to the countertop where Flynn darted out and began snarfing them down as if his belly wasn't distended enough. Denise didn't appear to notice him.

"Only he died," I supplied, taking another mouthful of cookie. "You wanna have a look around for the books?" I offered.

Denise looked at me hopefully. "Is that okay? You don't mind?"

"Not at all. There's the bookcase in the living room and another in the front bedroom upstairs. I'd offer to help, but you probably know better than me what you're looking for, and I need to start cleaning up this mess."

Denise reached out and grabbed my hand, clasping

it between both of hers. "Thank you so much," she gushed. "You have no idea what this means."

Uncomfortable at her gratitude, I pulled away, feeling my face heat. "Sure, sure, not a problem. Anytime." Which, of course, I didn't mean since I didn't relish having my privacy invaded.

Denise left for the living room with her half-demolished snickerdoodle, Flynn hot on her heels, no doubt hoping for more crumbs. I finished packing away the cookies, then washed the baking trays and mixing bowls before wiping down the counter tops. By the time I was done, Denise was upstairs, and Flynn had rejoined me in the kitchen, clearly deciding climbing the stairs was too much of an effort. I made myself a cup of coffee and sat on one of the kitchen chairs, sipping the piping hot brew while half-listening to Denise moving about, half-listening to the thunder and the sound of rain hitting the windows and roof.

My mind drifted as I pondered who had killed Seth and why. Which brought me around to thinking about my fake great uncle's death. An apparent suicide, yet most folks believed it wasn't, and with what Doris had told me about the missing ladder, I was inclined to agree with them. It niggled that I didn't want to think Calder had shoddy investigative skills, that I was searching around for other reasons as to why the death had been ruled a suicide rather than a homicide like so many people thought.

Two deaths. Months apart. Were they related? One

way to know for sure was to find out all I could about John's death, which meant asking for Calder's help. And no cop liked you poking around in a past case that had been closed, looking for holes in their investigation.

Reaching into my pocket, I pulled out the rune. I could return this to Calder on the pretense of asking him if anything similar had been found when John died. Maybe it had, and no one had given it a moment's thought. Like Doris had said, the police wouldn't know what to make of it, and it would end up languishing in an evidence bag.

Pulling out my phone, I dialed the second saved number.

He answered on the third ring. "Calder."

"Sorry to bother you. This is Holly Day—"

"Holly! Is everything okay?" he cut in before I'd finished speaking.

"Yes, I'm fine. Look." I cleared my throat and injected as much innocence into my tone as I could muster. "Remember that black rock we found in the barn? With Seth's body? Well, I just found it in my pocket! Honestly, I have no idea how it got there."

"So, that's where it got to. I thought Doris had pilfered it. I was going to visit her tomorrow." His tone was friendly, not irate, which was a positive sign.

That's when I realized how late it was getting. "Gosh, sorry, I didn't realize the time. I'm all out of whack today. Anyway, I'll let you go. I just wanted you to know that I have it. I can drop it into your office tomorrow if that helps?"

"Actually, I'm about to do my rounds, check on the town and how it's faring in this storm. If you're not heading to bed anytime soon, I'll drop in and pick it up. I'm going to need to get your prints to exclude you from the investigation anyway."

"My prints," I hedged. It would not be good to have my prints in the system.

"Since you've handled the evidence," he explained.

"Right. Of course." Darn. Now I would need to hack into the Gravestone PD database and delete my prints. Harding would not be pleased.

"I'll see you in an hour or so," Calder said before hanging up.

Overhead, a floorboard creaked, and I raised my eyes to the ceiling. "I forgot Denise was still here," I whispered to Flynn, wondering if she had overheard me talking to Calder about discovering Seth's body.

Flynn headed for the stairs while I stood and waited at the bottom.

"Everything okay up there?" I yelled.

I could just make out a startled gasp, then Denise called back, "Yes. Sorry, I won't be much longer."

"Maybe I should help." I put one foot on the bottom stair and was preparing to haul myself up when she appeared on the landing and smiled down at me, brandishing a book in her hand.

"No need, I found it!" She hustled down the stairs so fast she was a blur. She had the front door open and her umbrella ready before I was even halfway to the door. "Thanks so much. Sorry for the intrusion. See you later." And she was gone. The door stood open, and I gazed out into the dark, wet night. Of Denise Hurt, there was no sign.

CHAPTER

Fifteen

At ten pm on the dot, Calder pounded on my front door.

"You'd better make yourself scarce," I told Flynn, remembering Calder's reaction to the rat. "Just in case you startle him, and he takes another shot at you."

Flynn didn't need to be told twice, scampering up the stairs as fast as his fat little body would allow. I sincerely hoped eating all those cookies wasn't bad for his health.

Calder had his hat in his hands when I opened the door and stood back, inviting him inside. "Lovely weather," I joked, but Calder didn't so much as crack a smile. He twisted the hat in his fingers.

"The rock?" he prompted.

"Oh, sure. I put it in a Ziplock bag. It's in the kitchen." I led the way, my walking boot thumping in an off-beat rhythm across the floor. "I've been baking all evening. Want a snickerdoodle? They're proving to be quite popular."

"No thanks." He brushed past me when he spotted the Ziplock bag on the counter, the black pebble with the gold rune inside. Picking up the bag, he squinted through the plastic at the rune.

"Do you know what it means?" I asked. Of course, both Doris and I took photos of the rune and planned to look it up in Doris's books tomorrow. I'd be astonished if Calder had managed to unearth its meaning before we did.

"No. Do you?" His hazel eyes watched me intently.

I shrugged. "Nope." For once, it wasn't a lie. But I lied by omission. I knew the rune was a hex. A deadly one. Which meant that when the forensics came back on Seth Saltzman's body, they'd find no apparent cause of death. He hadn't been shot, stabbed, or strangled.

Calder shoved the plastic bag into his pocket, then eyeballed me.

"What?" I protested. "Are you mad I took it? Honestly, I don't remember taking it. It wasn't intentional. All I remember is touching it, and then my allergy kicked in. I have no idea what happened to it after that." *Lie, lie, lie.* He'd been right with his initial assessment that Doris had pilfered it.

Calder's chin rested on his chest as he let out a breath. I could only describe his expression when he lifted his head as resigned.

"There's been a tip-off," he said.

"There has?" *Fantastic. A lead.*

But his face said he didn't think the lead was all that fantastic. In fact, his face said the information was bad news. For me. Resigned, I sank onto a kitchen chair. "I'm not going to like it, am I?"

It was a rhetorical question, but he answered anyway. "Probably not." I caught the way his eyes shifted from me to the kitchen doorway and the staircase beyond. "Look. You can tell me to leave and get a warrant, or you can let me take a look around."

I rolled a shoulder and quirked a brow. "By all means. Look around. You've already searched this place once. Like I said, I've got nothing to hide." Except for the bones taped to the cedar elm in my back yard, but I hardly thought Calder intended to go tree climbing in this weather. No. Whatever the tip-off was, it was something inside this house.

"Thanks," he said gruffly, as if embarrassed he had to do this.

"Can I ask what the tip-off was?" First, the bones planted at my house, now a tip-off. Someone really didn't want me in Gravestone.

"I have to follow procedure," he hedged.

"Sure." I shrugged again. So, he wasn't going to tell me. Fine. I could live with that. When he headed for the stairs, I promptly got up and followed him. He went straight for the spare bedroom and my open suitcase on the floor. I stood watching while, with a pen, he began moving items of clothing around. Then he froze.

"What? What did you find?" I limped to his side and looked down into my trashed suitcase. I wasn't a particularly neat person, and rummaging through my suitcase on a daily basis had left it a red hot mess. He pointed, and I crouched by his side, leaning forward to get a closer look.

"What? That pen?" I was aghast. *The evidence was a pen?* "That's not even mine," I added.

Retrieving an evidence bag from his back pocket, he shook it open and then scooped up the pen, sealing it inside the bag before holding it aloft.

"Gold Posca paint pen," he announced.

"Appears to be." I nodded in agreement. "And the relevance?"

"Same type of pen used to make the markings on the rock."

"The rock that I only just gave to you? The one we found last night with Seth's body? The same one no one else knows about?"

He nodded. "The same."

"And you know that that makes no sense. How can you possibly have a tip-off about evidence you haven't examined or logged yet, let alone forensically identify the marker used?"

That's when he smiled, and my insides did a flip-flop. An honest to God somersault. Taken aback, I lost my balance and toppled onto my butt. While Matt Casey was eye candy personified, Joshua Calder had a rugged handsomeness impossible to ignore. I resisted the urge to fan myself, cursing my hormones for deciding to wake up at precisely the wrong moment.

"Hey, you okay there?" Shoving the evidence bag

into his jeans pocket, he stood, reaching out to help me to my feet. As soon as his hands closed over mine, a zap of electricity shot across my skin, making my heart skip and my breath catch in my throat. I stood there, hands in his, heart beating double time, lost for words.

"Holly?" he quizzed, bending to peer into my eyes. "You sure you're okay?"

Tugging my hands from his, I took a step back and sucked in a deep breath. "Yeah. Sure. Sorry." Clearing my throat, I indicated my suitcase. "I assume you're thinking the same thing I am. That someone planted that evidence in an attempt to make me look guilty."

"Yep. But what that person didn't know was that I didn't have the rock with the symbol drawn onto it in evidence yet, so I hadn't examined it."

"So, you wouldn't have discovered that the symbol was drawn with a gold Posca pen. Which is oddly specific."

I led the way from the bedroom and back down the stairs. "You didn't mention any of this when I called." I was thinking out loud. "Which means the tip-off didn't come in until… what? After nine?"

"Ten past," Calder confirmed.

I stopped and turned. "I'm guessing you're not going to find any prints on that pen. So, it's purely circumstantial that it was found in my suitcase."

"Correct on both counts." Rather than heading toward the front door, he headed for the kitchen. "Any chance of getting some coffee?"

"Oh! Sure. Want a snickerdoodle to go with that?"

"If it tastes anything like this kitchen smells, then yes, please." His grin was back, and I really didn't know what to make of it. I was used to Calder grumbling and being annoyed with me, not this sense of camaraderie I felt between us.

I busied myself pouring coffee from the almost empty pot. "I find it very interesting that you got a call just after nine with a tip-off that I have evidence tied to Seth Seltzman's murder," I said. "Because I had three unexpected visitors this evening between eight and nine, and any one of them could have planted that pen."

"Who?" Calder was all business, taking a seat at the table and pulling out a small notepad to make a note of what I was about to tell him.

"Matt Casey dropped in to check on the roof."

"Not unusual for Casey to do something like that."

"Exactly what I thought," I agreed. "Especially as I'm hiring him to do some repairs to this place."

"Who else?"

"The mayor. Kerris Jones." I glanced over my shoulder, keen to observe Calder's reaction to the mayor's visit. He didn't disappoint, his brows shooting up, his head cocking to the side.

"The mayor? What did she want?"

"To offer me an outrageous sum of money to sell her this house."

"And it couldn't wait until morning? She had to come out in a storm?"

"I asked myself those same questions."

"Did you answer yourself?" he teased.

"Actually," I tapped a finger to my lower lip, "I'm wondering if she didn't want anyone to know she was here. The storm is the perfect cover."

"Hmmm. Plausible, I guess. Did she have the opportunity to plant the pen?"

"She did go upstairs to use the bathroom, which I found odd in itself, given she'd just been screeching at me about how unhygienic it is to keep a pet rat and that she'd have this place condemned."

At the mention of Flynn, Calder glanced around uneasily.

"Relax. He's sleeping somewhere. He's no more keen to be shot at than you are."

Calder lowered his head and cleared his throat. "Sorry about that. So, who was the third person?"

"Denise Hurt. Apparently, John had promised to lend her a book on the history of Gravestone."

"And coming out in a storm seemed like the perfect time to collect it?" Calder drawled.

"I figured maybe since the weather was bad, it gave her something to do?" I shrugged, placing a coffee in front of Calder along with the container of snickerdoodle's. "Was the voice male or female? The tip-off," I added when he looked at me, confused.

"Disguised. One of those voice synthesizer things."

Compressing my lips, I cradled my coffee and sat opposite Calder, lost in thought.

"I'll get warrants for phone records tomorrow,"

Calder said. "Assuming that whoever called in the tip-off used their own phone and not a burner."

"In the meantime, there's actually something I wanted to ask you."

"Oh?" He took a mouthful of snickerdoodle and rolled his eyes. "This is good!"

"You don't have to sound so surprised," I complained.

"I meant it as a compliment."

Not used to receiving compliments, I decided the best course of action was to ignore it. "I wanted to ask you about John Smith's death."

"What about it?"

"I heard it was ruled a suicide, but almost everyone I've spoken to doesn't believe that."

Calder stopped chewing and stared at me for a full five seconds before his jaw started working again.

"I was on vacation," he stated, voice devoid of any hint of emotion. "I didn't handle the case. From what I've seen and heard, it was open and shut."

"I don't mean to imply anything," I reassured him. "But I'm sorry, I just don't see how a man of John's age and physical limitations could haul himself into that tree and hang himself. And Doris tells me his ladder is missing."

"His ladder?"

"Yes. We talked about how it is improbable John climbed that tree. If he did hang himself, the logical way would be to use a ladder—or a chair—but a ladder makes more sense because the branch he was found hanging from is high off the ground. Anyway, if you were going to kill yourself, you'd use a ladder, throw the rope over, secure it around your neck, then kick the ladder away."

"Only there was no ladder," Calder said.

"No ladder," I agreed. "But again, I'm only going on what Doris told me. Could you check the report?" If I could convince Calder to examine John Smith's suicide, maybe, just maybe, we'd learn if a rune had been left on his body too.

"I'll look into it."

CHAPTER
Sixteen

Doris, hair in curlers, floral nightie visible beneath her knee-length coat, dripped water on my living room floor while looking at me askance.

"Say that again," she demanded, lifting one foot out of the black Wellington boots that were three sizes too big. "Someone planted evidence to implicate you in Seth's death?"

"You heard me. I called Calder to tell him I had the rune—don't worry, I covered for you. He said he was going to patrol the town and drop by to pick it up. Then he received an anonymous tip-off that I had…well, I'm not exactly sure what the tip-off said, but anyway, it was enough for Calder to ask to look around. He went straight to my suitcase and found the gold pen apparently used to draw the rune on the rock."

"You're not languishing in a cell, so I take it he doesn't believe you're guilty?" Doris stepped out of the other boot, leaving it abandoned in the living room while she headed to the kitchen, shrugging out of the coat as she went, dropping it onto the back of a chair to drip water on the kitchen floor. Why not? I already had puddles in the living room. May as well add the kitchen to the mix.

"Considering I still had the rune in my possession, and therefore no forensic testing had been done, no. Not to mention I wasn't even in town when Seth died. And he's agreed to take a look at John Smith's case."

"That's a lot. This is going to require caffeine," she said, grabbing the freshly replenished pot and grinning like a loon. "Glad you have a pot going. It's like you already know me."

"I know me," I said, sliding my cup across the counter for a refill. "And I agree. This definitely requires caffeine." Let's disregard the fact that I'd burned through one pot of coffee already this evening and had the tremor in my hands to prove it.

"So, what you're saying is someone has been in your house and has planted evidence?"

"Correct." I'd sent Doris a text as soon as Calder had left, advising her of the latest development. She'd promptly arrived on my doorstep.

Pouring the coffee, her brow furrowed in concentration, Doris appeared deep in thought. I remained silent, giving her time to get her gray cells working. She was silent for so long I thought she'd fallen asleep standing up.

"Everything okay there?" I prompted.

Doris jumped, then waved a hand in dismissal

before filling both cups and sliding mine back across the counter. "Here you go. Which brings me to my second point."

"There was a first?" I grinned, taking my cup and resuming my seat at the kitchen table. Doris plopped down in the chair opposite.

"My point is, who is crazy enough to be out in this weather?" She cocked her head toward the kitchen window, and we watched the rivulets of water streaming over the glass. Every now and then, a flash of lightning lit up the sky, followed by the low rumble of thunder. It had been storming for hours with no sign of letting up anytime soon.

"The only visit that made any sense was Casey. He dropped by to check on the roof, to make sure it wasn't leaking."

"So, obviously, he went upstairs. Did you go with him?"

I shook my head. "No. I was baking. He wasn't up there long."

"It doesn't take long to stash evidence in your suitcase," she pointed out. "And you can't deny Casey has a motive for killing Seth."

"Because of River." I nodded. But even then, the motive was flimsy. Seth and River had been dating for six months before Seth was killed. If this were a crime of passion and Casey the perpetrator, surely he'd have acted sooner? Or maybe discovering that Seth was cheating on River and stealing from the town was what pushed him over the edge?

"What about John Smith? It seems that Casey admired him, a fellow carpenter and all that. Why choose him as his next victim?" I was sure the deaths were related.

"What were you baking?"

"What?"

"When Casey dropped by. You said you were baking."

"Oh! Snickerdoodle's. Want one?"

Doris's face split into a wide grin, the crow's feet at the corners of her eyes deepening. I leaned backward in my chair, grabbed the snickerdoodle's container from the bench, and passed it to her.

"I don't think Casey is our man," she said, cracking the lid and helping herself to a cookie. I was inclined to agree.

"That leaves Kerris and Denise." Best focus on the remaining suspects. It had to be one of the women. Kerris was my top suspect. She obviously wanted this house. Did she kill John Smith to get it, only me turning up ruined her plans? As for Seth, maybe she'd donated money to his fundraiser and was furious when the truth came out.

"What did Kerris want?" Doris asked, taking a bite of her snickerdoodle.

"To offer me an obscene amount of money to buy this place." I told her what Kerris had offered, and Doris's eyes bugged out on stalks.

"You should have taken the offer!" she cried.

Clearing my throat, I pointed out, "You forget that

this house isn't really mine to sell. John Smith isn't really my great uncle. It's an SIA cover story."

Doris waved a hand in dismissal. "Semantics."

"Illegal."

"How did she get upstairs?"

I frowned. "The usual means. She used the staircase."

Doris guffawed. "No, silly. I mean, what reason did she have for going upstairs?"

"Oh, right! To use the bathroom."

Doris's eyebrows disappeared beneath the curler holding the white hair off her forehead. "Kerris Jones used your bathroom?"

I shrugged. "When you gotta pee, you gotta pee."

"Yes, but she has… standards."

"And you're saying I don't?" Actually, it was a fair call. I'd been in worst dives than this and had never batted an eye. And the way Kerris had carried on about health violations and having me shut down hardly fit the profile of someone prepared to use my facilities.

"I'm saying Kerris Jones would never, in a million years, use the bathroom in a dump like this. No offense. She was either snooping or planting evidence."

"What about Denise Hurt?" Our last suspect. "Could she be the killer? Is she one of yours?"

"Denise is a member of the Gravestone Women's Committee, yes." Doris nodded. "Quiet thing, keeps to herself."

"So, she's a witch?"

Doris shrugged. "Not that she's ever admitted to me."

I was taken aback. "So, she's *not* one of yours?"

With a heartfelt sigh, and using the same tone of voice you'd use with a three-year-old, Doris explained, "The Gravestone Women's Committee is *not* a coven. There are no covens in Gravestone. Gravestone is on a ley line that obscures magic. What would be the point if we were all out in the open, flouting it? That's why your boss sent you here. To hide you."

"He also told me not to use my magic so it couldn't be traced."

"An added precaution. Sounds to me like your boss is a very wise man."

I narrowed my eyes. "You're sure you don't know him? Scott Harding," I reminded her.

"Nope. Never heard of him." It pained me to admit I had no idea if she was telling the truth or lying.

A flash of lightning lit up my back yard, followed a scant second later by a clap of thunder so loud it shook the house. Then the lights went out. Doris and I sat in the dark, our breaths the only sound over the continuing patter of rain.

"Excellent," Doris said. I couldn't see her face to tell if she was being sarcastic or not.

"It is?" I rummaged under the sink for my newly purchased flashlight.

"The power is out. Probably be out for a while. My guess is a lightning strike on the power lines."

"Right." I nodded. "And this is excellent because?"

"Because Kerris Jones's alarm system will be off."

"And why is that important?" I don't know why I bothered asking, for I had a hunch I knew exactly what Doris was thinking. Truth be told, as soon as we'd been plunged into darkness, the exact same thought had skittered across my brain. Now would be an excellent time to break into Kerris Jones's house and find the evidence I needed. The storm would provide a most outstanding cover. Just like she'd used the storm to hide the fact she'd visited me, I would turn the tables and do the same.

Doris jumped to her feet, the chair legs scraping across the floor in protest. Shoving the rest of the snickerdoodle in her mouth, she mumbled through the mouthful of cookie, "Let's go! There's shenanigans to be had."

***

Creeping up Kerris Jones's driveway in the pitch dark in the middle of a thunderstorm was not the craziest thing I'd ever done. That would have involved an elf with a predilection for ale who rode a wilderbeast for transport. We'd shared an eventful evening in Las Vegas, both on the same case, only the elf had beaten me to the punch by incapacitating the perp with a stiletto through the temple. That's where Bounty and SIA differed. SIA liked me to bring perps in alive. Bounty would take 'em either way.

We'd hatched a plan on the drive over. Doris would

be the lookout. With her black mackintosh-style raincoat and oversized boots, she would hide in the shadows and create a distraction if needed. I'd boost it over the back fence and let myself in via the doggie door. Doris had assured me that Kerris's dog, Jasper, would be cowering inside, fearful of the storm. He'd be no problem at all. A pussy cat. Which was a relief because I didn't relish coming face to face with an angry German shepherd. Flynn and I would search the house for anything that would implicate Kerris.

"Well?" Doris hissed. "What are you waiting for? Over you go." She gave me a shove toward the six-foot fence surrounding Kerris's back yard.

"Remember the plan?" I straightened the makeshift garbage bag poncho I was currently wearing. I wasn't averse to discomfort, but it was still hot, and I was slowly steaming alive beneath the unforgiving plastic despite the rain. But it was either the poncho or be soaked to the skin. A second bag encased my walking boot.

"Yes. If there's some sort of ruckus, I'm to knock on the front door and say my car has broken down and ask for help." We'd parked Doris's car around the corner, out of sight but close enough for a relatively quick getaway if needed.

"Right." Placing my hands on top of the fence, I pulled myself up and over, dropping into a crouch on the other side, my bum leg sticking out at an awkward angle. Flynn was hanging from my hair like an oversized dreadlock.

"All good?" Doris whispered from the other side.

"All good."

I waited, listening as Doris shuffled away, taking up her position behind the elm in Kerris's front garden. We'd spotted a flickering light in the living room window and assumed that was where Kerris was waiting out the storm and power outage. I had a scrawled map of the layout of her house. Now it was just a matter of getting in, finding the evidence that would implicate her in the murders, and getting out again without being discovered. Easy peasy. I could do it in my sleep.

I crept down the side of the house to the rear. Between one strike of lightning and another, I had enough light to see, quickly finding my way to the doggie door Doris had told me about. Cautiously, I pushed it open and, scooping Flynn into my hand, shoved him inside before poking my head through. The doggie door opened into a mud room, complete with a dog bed and food bowls. Both empty.

Wriggling the rest of my body through the door, I slowly rose to my full height, water dripping from my makeshift poncho. I shook off as much as I could in the mud room and wiped my feet on the doormat. If Kerris noticed the droplets of water, she'd assume Jasper had ducked outside for a potty break. That's what I hoped anyway.

Flynn darted out of the mud room ahead of me and scurried down the hallway. It was almost pitch black as I inched my way along the wall. Every now and then,

I'd come to an open doorway, and a flash of lightning would provide a brief moment of clarity before plunging everything into darkness again.

A sharp nip on my ankle had me hissing in a breath. It was Flynn, trying to tell me something, but of course, I couldn't even see him, let alone try and work out what he wanted. Dropping to my hands and knees, I whispered, "guide me," and with one hand resting on his back, I awkwardly crawled the length of the hallway until we reached the room at the end. The master suite. Kerris's bedroom.

Once inside, I pushed the door, so it was almost closed but not latched, then pulled the flashlight from the waistband of my shorts. Kerris's bedroom was exactly what I'd imagined it to be. Opulent. Lots of glass, crystal, and mirrors. The bed was covered in dozens of throw pillows, and a lace embellished comforter dangled over the sides. On almost every available surface were small figurines of dogs. Hundreds of them.

"She's a dog lover, all right," I whispered to Flynn, who had climbed up the side of the bed and was now sniffing around her pillows. She'd have a conniption if she knew a rat was not only in her room but on her pillow. Creeping across the room, I opened the door to her closet, freezing when the door creaked. Flynn and I both looked to the door, listening, but no footsteps approached. No one had heard us. Thankfully the rumbling thunder and never-ending rain provided enough noise to cover any sounds we made.

A quick search of Kerris's bedroom turned up nothing. Nothing remotely witch-crafty, and no Posca paint pens, let alone black rocks waiting to be adorned with runes. Pulling out the map scrawled on a napkin, I studied it. Kerris's house had three bedrooms. Doris was pretty sure Kerris used one as a home office. She assumed the other was a guest room. Time to find out.

Creeping out of the master bedroom, I headed across the hallway to the second bedroom, and as predicted, it was set up as a home office. Unlike her very feminine bedroom, the office was all dark mahogany and clean, masculine lines. No doggie figurines here. There was a desk lamp, a tray with a few papers waiting for her attention, a laptop, and a pen. Not a Posca. A quick search of the drawers turned up nothing of interest, although my eyes lingered on a folder marked *boardwalk*. Opening the file, I laid the enclosed papers across the desk and snapped photos before returning them to the file and closing the drawer. I'd examine these later and find out precisely what Kerris was up to with her outrageous offer on the house and her proposed boardwalk.

Leaving the office, I headed toward the third bedroom. The door was slightly ajar, and I eased inside, holding the flashlight aloft to reveal Kerris had turned this room into a craft room. A sewing machine sat on a white counter along one wall. The shelf above it held a collection of cotton threads. In the center of the room, another table with cube shelving beneath it dominated.

In each cube was a rattan basket. Keeping as quiet as possible, I began pulling out each basket.

"Jeez, this woman must love her crafting," I whispered to Flynn, who was poking around in the bolts of fabric stacked on a bookcase next to the sewing machine. Each basket held odds and ends depending on what Kerris was working on. There were items for knitting, painting, cross-stitch, flower pressing, mixed media—you name it, it appeared Kerris Jones had it.

When I pulled out the basket with the Posca paint pens, my heart stuttered, then resumed beating a mile a minute. "Here!" I hissed to Flynn. In the basket were dozens upon dozens of pens. It was impossible to tell if she was missing a gold one, for they were loose in the basket.

"See if she has any black rocks or pebbles," I instructed.

Flynn immediately began scampering over and in each basket, burying his nose deep and rummaging around. We were still searching when my phone vibrated, and a text message appeared.

"*You need to get out of there. Now!*" Doris wrote.

"We need to go," I whispered to Flynn, whose head appeared from one of the baskets. Flynn looked at me, then beyond me. His ears flattened, and his fur stood on end. "What is it?"

He raised a paw and pointed, and slowly, I turned my head. There, in the doorway, stood Jasper, the German shepherd.

"Nice puppy," I soothed, slowly moving my hand to

rest on the basket so Flynn could clamber on board. As soon as he was settled on my shoulder, I inched toward the door, not meeting Jasper's eyes, trying to reassure the dog I was no threat.

"Jasper, darling? Where are you?" Kerris called, and I froze.

Jasper barked. Then barked again.

Holy crapadoodles. We were about to be busted in the worst way. There was nowhere to hide in the craft room, and with the dog in the hallway, blocking my exit to the doggy door, I had to find another hiding spot, fast.

Flynn tugged on my hair and pointed his little rat arm. The master bedroom. We could at least hide out in the closet. I prayed we wouldn't be stuck there all night.

"What is it, boy?" Kerris called. She was still in the living room, but if Jasper barked again, I was pretty sure she'd come to investigate. As I approached the craft room door, the dog retreated. Could I get him to withdraw all the way back to the mud room door, giving us access to the exit?

I was in the hallway, two steps toward the mud room, when Jasper found his backbone and held his ground. Planting his front paws, he lowered his head and growled.

"Shoot," I cursed under my breath. "Plan B. Back to the bedroom." I backed up slowly, one hand trailing along the wall to guide me as I shuffled awkwardly in my boot, the plastic poncho crinkling and sounding impossibly loud.

My phone vibrated, but I didn't have time to look at it. The dog was barring our escape, and if Doris had told us to get out, it meant another threat was looming. There was no recourse except to hide. Thankfully, Jasper stayed where he was while Flynn and I slowly backed down the hallway and into Kerris's bedroom. Lucky for us, he'd stopped barking. I'd no sooner thought it than the unthinkable happened. One *woof* was all it took, and Jasper put all he had into it, the bark echoing down the hallway and bouncing off the walls.

With no time to spare, I flung myself to the floor and rolled under Kerris's bed with Flynn attached to my scalp, holding on for dear life. From beneath the bed and lace frill of the comforter, I watched as Kerris's flashlight lit up the hallway.

"What's up, boy?" she asked, standing beside the dog. Jasper trotted down the hallway toward the bedroom, and Kerris laughed. "You think it's time for bed, huh?"

I could feel my phone vibrating in my pocket. Message after message, no doubt from Doris telling me to get the heck out of there. I didn't dare reach for it, though. Any movement may set Jasper off, alerting Kerris that she had intruders in her bedroom.

My eyes widened in horror when her feet began moving toward the bed, and for the briefest of moments, I thought she'd heard us, but rather than kneeling down and peering under the bed, she sat on it. The mattress sagged, and the slats creaked in protest. I sucked in a breath, hoping the wooden slats currently under strain would hold. Another horrifying thought crossed my mind... what if she decided to go to sleep? I mean, it made perfect sense, right? The power was out, a storm was raging, what else were you going to do? Plus, it was getting late.

Flynn released his death grip on my scalp and crawled across my face; in his wake, a smell that made my nose twitch, then burn. My eyes began to water as the stench assaulting me took full effect. *He'd farted.* Flynn had crawled across my face and farted. It took every ounce of self-control not to move, to breathe through my mouth as quietly as possible while the toxic gas cloud he'd left behind singed my nostril hairs and stripped the enamel from my teeth. No more snickerdoodle's for him if this is what they did! Beneath my struggle for oxygen lay a genuine concern for Flynn's health—surely a rodent his size was incapable of producing such a toxic gas cloud?

Just when I thought I'd be forced to crawl out from my hiding spot to seek fresh air, a banging on the front door drew our attention.

"Who could that be on a night like this?" Kerris asked Jasper. Jasper let out a woof and trotted out of the room, Kerris following.

"Thank God," I whispered, rolling out from beneath the bed, Flynn leading the way. "That must be Doris. Let's get out of here."

I was creeping down the hallway toward the mud room when my blood froze in my veins. The voice at the front door was not Doris's. It was Calder's!

"Sheriff," Kerris greeted. "What brings you by on such an awful night? Not that you need an excuse to visit. You're always welcome."

I cringed at the seductive tone and could just imagine her preening in front of the sheriff. Calder was all business. "I'm dropping in to check that y'all are okay here with the blackout. Doing my duty."

"Everything is fine, although poor Jasper is spooked." The dog whined at the mention of his name, then barked, then the sounds of his paws heading our way.

"We've gotta move!" I hissed to Flynn, although I needn't have bothered. He was nowhere in sight. Thankfully, the next door I came to was the mudroom, and I dove for the doggie door, pushing through headfirst, my momentum forcing me through the door with no wriggling required. I executed a perfect somersault landing, but in my haste, I'd made more noise than intended, and Jasper sounded off like a car alarm, drawing attention to our hasty retreat.

I spotted Flynn ahead, sprinting for the corner of the house. I followed, my walking boot slowing me down. I'd just cleared the corner of the house when I heard the back door open and caught a glimpse of a flashlight sweeping across the yard.

Flynn squeezed through a gap under the fence, but I had no such luxury; instead, I jumped, hauled myself over, and landed with a thump on the other side. I could only hope the wind, rain, and thunder masked the unholy racket I made. I glanced over to the elm where Doris was hiding, only she wasn't there. Heart thundering, I headed toward the tree. With any luck, Calder and Kerris would remain at the back of the house for a few more minutes, giving me time to either get clear or hide.

I'd just reached the big elm, pressing my back to the bark while I caught my breath, when a car came barreling up the street, headlights out. Taking a gamble it was Doris, I launched away from the tree and sprinted as fast as my busted foot would allow toward the road. The Impala screeched to a halt, and I jumped into the passenger seat, Flynn leaping in after me to land on my lap.

"Go," I hissed. Doris didn't need telling twice, pulling away before I'd closed the door. We shot past Calder's truck, and twisting in my seat, I just made out the front door of Kerris's house opening, and then we were at the end of the street and out of view.

"That was close." Doris grinned.

"Turn on the lights," I reminded her as soon as we were clear of Kerris's house.

"Well? Find anything?" she asked.

I nodded. "A whole basket full of Posca paint pens. No way of knowing if the one found at my house came from her stash, though. And no rocks, although we didn't get a chance to finish searching."

"I did send you a warning," Doris said, as if defending herself from my non-existent censure.

"I got it. Thanks," I assured her with a pat on the shoulder. "We had trouble with Jasper."

"Ooooh. Should have taken a snickerdoodle with you."

I pulled out my phone and checked my messages while Doris drove us back to my house. As suspected, all of them were from Doris.

"Abort."

"Abort. Abort. ABORT."

"What are you waiting for? Get out of there!"

"Holy heck."

"Plan B."

"There was a plan B?" I asked, glancing up from the final message.

Doris shrugged. "I was going to pull in behind Calder and hit the horn. I'd just driven around the corner when I saw you on the lawn." We were silent for the remainder of the drive home until, sitting in front of my house with the engine idling, Doris said, "We need to finish searching. The pens aren't enough to incriminate her, but if we find a black rock?"

"One tiny flaw in your plan. She's at home, and her dog, Jasper, was somewhat of a problem."

"So, we wait until she's not home."

"Assuming by then that the power will be back on and, therefore, her alarm system," I pointed out.

"We'll burn that bridge when we get to it."

I snorted out a laugh. "Let's regroup tomorrow. You'd best get home in case Calder decides it's a good idea to check in on us too."

Seventeen

Calder didn't check on us. Despite having slept more than sixteen hours the night before, I'd fallen asleep as soon as my head hit the pillow and didn't stir until the pounding on my front door woke me the following morning.

"Yes?" I opened the door in the shorts and tank I'd slept in, my hair a mess and morning breath leaving a horrid taste in my mouth.

"Good morning, sunshine." Doris beamed, bustling past me and heading for the kitchen. I looked outside. The storm had cleared, the morning dawned with clear skies and a skyrocketing temperature. There was no sign of the Impala.

"What time is it?" I grumbled, closing the door and following Doris into the kitchen. "And where's your car?"

"I walked." She shrugged and thumped her bag onto the kitchen counter.

"Walked? Why?"

"No reason." She wouldn't meet my eyes, instead busying herself with the coffee pot. Thankfully, the power had been restored while I'd slept. "Can't a girl get a little exercise without being interrogated?"

"Your car broke down, didn't it?" I guessed. "What was it? Left the lights on, and now your battery is dead?"

She sniffed. "Maybe." Straightening her shoulders, she squinted at me. "Why don't you go freshen up? Heaven knows you look like you've been pulled through a bramble bush backward. I'll take care of the coffee."

"Fine." I ran upstairs to splash water on my face and run a brush through my hair. Flynn followed me, sitting on the hand basin, scooping little pawfuls of water from the running faucet and splashing his face. This morning, his fur was yellow.

"What is it with that?" I murmured, pulling my hair into a ponytail and securing it with an elastic band. Flynn shrugged, continuing his morning bath while I went to rummage in my suitcase for something clean to wear. I was going to have to do laundry soon, or buy some new clothes, for the amount of sweating I was doing in Gravestone was beyond ridiculous.

Pulling on a pair of jeans and a black tank, slightly wrinkled, I returned to the bathroom to turn off the faucet, ignored Flynn's squeak of protest, and headed back downstairs to find Doris sitting at the kitchen table sipping from a steaming cup of coffee.

Sitting opposite her, I strapped my boot on over my jeans and picked up the coffee she'd made me, taking a hefty gulp. Much better. Now I felt semi-alive and reasonably coherent.

"Did you manage to work out what the rune meant?" I asked.

Doris shook her head. "Nothing like it in my grimoire. Although it probably doesn't matter what it means. We know it's a death hex. What else is there to know?"

"Origins might be helpful," I suggested. "Did you know Kerris is a witch?"

"It does make sense," Doris admitted. "How she become mayor, how she manages to manipulate every situation to her favor."

"You think she's been using magic all this time? Like for the vote with the Women's Committee? River seemed surprised Kerris won."

"Exactly."

"That reminds me. I found a file about the boardwalk in Kerris's office. I took photos. Let me get my phone." My phone was where I'd left it on the floor in the living room next to the cot. Picking it up, I frowned when I realized I had a message from Calder. Odd that I hadn't heard it ding. Opening the message, my eyes widened.

"*This was found in your uncle's pocket,*" he wrote, and attached was a photograph of a black rock with a gold rune painted on it.

"Oh, my God, Doris, look!" I hobbled back into the

kitchen and held out my phone to her so she could see the photo. "Calder just sent me this," I explained. "It was found in John Smith's pocket."

"It's the same," we said in unison.

"I'm sure to the police it was just a rock with some squiggles drawn on it. Inconsequential," Doris said.

"Agreed. I wonder if Calder could get me a copy of John's autopsy report?"

"Why not ask him? He sent you that." She jerked her head at the photo on my phone. "So, he's open to you at least asking."

I chewed my lip. "Yeah, but we're also withholding evidence. We have Seth's bones taped to a tree. How can I get them back to Calder without implicating myself? Or you?"

Doris snapped her fingers. "I've got it! We put the bones back where we found them and then call Calder, saying they just turned up. Which is true, they did just turn up, only it was a couple of days ago—he doesn't need to know that part. He's already on board that someone is trying to frame you. This backs that up."

"You know, for a terrible idea, it's not bad."

"Right. Fancy a bit of tree climbing?"

I lifted my leg to reveal the walking boot.

"Oh, yeah, forgot about that. Looks like I'm it."

Flynn led the way with Doris and I following behind. We were closer to revealing Kerris was the witch behind the killings, but it niggled at me that I didn't find anything definitive at her house. Sure, she had a basket full of markers, but they were a common item, and given her predilection for crafting, it was hardly surprising. No, what I needed was proof she was a witch.

"What are you thinking about so hard? You look like you need a good dose of prunes," Doris said, coming to a halt at the base of the cedar elm.

I sighed. "I was thinking about Kerris," I admitted. "She has to be behind this. It's the only thing that makes sense."

"She's power hungry that's for sure," Doris agreed, spitting on her hands and rubbing them together. "Give me a boost will you?"

Cupping my hands together, I made a cradle for Doris's foot. She placed her right foot in it, and I boosted her to the first branch of the big old tree.

"Flynn, go with her, will you? She'll probably need help getting the tape undone."

Flynn nodded and shot up the tree behind her.

"Do you think Kerris really used magic to get elected?" I asked.

"Possibly."

"I didn't find anything in her house though." Which led me to believe Kerris practiced her magic somewhere else. Which of course made sense. As mayor, she no doubt had people visiting her house all the time. She most likely entertained there too. Which meant she wouldn't want anyone accidentally stumbling across anything incriminating. No… she'd have her grimoire and anything else she used in her ceremonies sequestered away somewhere else.

"Where would you hide your grimoire and ceremonial items?" I said out loud.

"You know the best hiding spot is in plain sight." Doris called down to me. I could no longer see her but could track her progress by the rustling of the leaves.

"True. But Kerris would hardly stash those items at work. Does she own any other property in town?"

"Besides being keen to get her hand on John's place, and old Reggie's next door, nope."

I turned and looked toward Reginald York's house, barely visible through the tree line. An old, abandoned house would certainly fit the bill. And maybe that's why John was targeted too, because he was convenient and lived in close proximity.

"Got them!" Doris yelled. "Here, Flynn, take these will you."

Flynn appeared moments later, the plastic bag with the bones dangling from his mouth, a trail of duct tape following behind. Doris shimmied down behind him.

"Right. We need to put them on the doorstep and then call Calder," I said.

"Kerris has already proven she can waltz straight into the police station and take whatever she wants," Doris reminded me.

"Although I'd imagine Calder has tightened security since that happened. Let's stick with the original plan. I can't keep the bones hidden here forever."

"Can't you?"

"Doris! No. I can't. Seth's bones need to be reunited so he can be buried in one piece."

Doris mumbled under her breath, something about Seth being lower than a snake's belly in a wagon rut and that he deserved to rest in pieces. Shaking my head, I followed Flynn inside. Unwrapping the bones, I placed them outside my front door and then disposed of the plastic bag and tape in the kitchen bin.

"There!" I declared, dusting my hands together. "Now to call Calder."

"Why not just leave them there for whoever comes to your door next to discover?" Doris suggested. "Distances you a little."

"That hardly seems fair," I protested. "What if it's Ada? She'll vomit all over them."

Doris chuckled, no doubt imagining Ada doing just that. "Fair call. Perhaps you should call Calder."

Pulling out my phone, I dialed, only it went to messages.

"Calder, hi, it's Holly Day. This is going to sound weird but… Seth's hand has just turned up on my front doorstep. Don't worry, I haven't touched anything, but I figured you'd want to know. Um. Okay. Thanks. Bye."

I hung up and looked at Doris, who was nodding her head as if to say *job well done*.

"Now what?" she asked.

"I want to check out Reggie's house." I pointed. "It's been empty for years, so Kerris could be using it for her spells."

Heading out the back door, the three of us skirted behind the trees separating John and Reggie's properties and approached from the rear of the house. If

I'd thought John's house had fallen into rack and ruin, it had nothing on Reggie's. Disrepair didn't cover it. The house looked… weirdly still standing. Goosebumps rose on my arms, and I shivered.

"I think this is the place," I whispered, spooked.

"You feel it, huh?" Doris whispered back. Even Flynn's fur was standing on end.

"Is it magic?"

"It's certainly a sense of foreboding. Probably a spell to keep people away," Doris suggested, easing forward through the weeds and approaching the back porch. The wood was buckled in places, missing in others, but there in the dust on the top step was a discernible foot print. Someone had definitely been inside recently.

"Get behind me," I hissed, shoving Doris behind me. Flynn streaked ahead, finding his way inside the house via the broken window next to the back door. I froze when I heard a latch turn, then the door was slowly swinging open. With my heart hammering in my chest, I bent my knees and raised my hands, prepared to fight, only it was Flynn balanced on the door handle.

"Smart rat," Doris said, nodding in approval.

I'm not going to lie, it was with a certain level of trepidation that I stepped over the threshold and into Reginald York's house.

"That's better," Doris said from behind me, and I had to agree. Now that we were inside, the sense of doom and foreboding had gone.

"Definitely magic," I agreed. Reggie's house was empty, save for dust and cobwebs. The floorboards creaked as Doris and I made our way through the kitchen and into the living room.

"Bingo!" Doris pointed toward two wooden crates pushed against the far wall, a plank of wood placed on top to create a makeshift table. Or altar. We hurried over. There, on the top of the altar, were three black rocks, a gold pen, and a scrap of paper. Picking up the paper, I squinted at it in the dim light peeking through the boarded over windows.

"This looks like a shopping list." I frowned, puzzled.

"For magical items?" Doris asked.

"No. Eggs, bread, milk. That sort of thing. But…" I held up the shopping list and studied it. "I've seen this writing before, I'm sure of it. The way she's written the 'a' with that little curl is quite unique."

"You know who writes her a's like that?" Doris piped up.

"Not Kerris."

"Denise Hurt," we said in unison, looking at each other in horror. I was so sure our murderous witch had been Kerris Jones that I was trying to shoehorn the evidence to fit. Only Kerris wasn't our killer.

"Ladies." Denise's voice from behind us had us both jumping a solid foot in the air. I spun to find Denise holding Flynn aloft by the scruff of his neck.

"Denise," Doris began, her voice scalding, "what is all this? What do you think you're doing? And for goodness sake, put that rat down. You don't know what you might catch."

"Nice try, but I know he's your familiar, Holly. Is your name even Holly?"

I nodded. "Yup. Holly Day." No way I was going to reveal my true identity to her. Denise Hurt, the sweet looking, mild-mannered senior in her floral dress, apron adorned with kittens, hair set in demure curls—although how she got curls to hold in this humidity must be witchcraft in itself—looked at me with murder in her eyes.

I looked at Doris. "How did we miss this?" I asked.

Doris threw her hands in the air. "Beats me. I was sure it was Kerris!"

"Me too!"

"Stop it!" Denise shouted, stamping a foot. We looked at her, eyes wide.

Yeah, sweet little Denise was a little bit unhinged. I could see it now, the way her eyes darted around the room as if unsure what she should focus on, the blush of color in her cheeks, the beads of sweat on her forehead. Although, granted, it was a thousand degrees in the old house, with zero air flow.

"You get that when dabbling in dark magic," Doris whispered out of the corner of her mouth.

"Can you read my mind?" I asked, louder than intended.

"No, honey. You've really got to teach your facial expressions how to use their inside face."

"Oh."

"Quiet!" Denise screeched, pulling back her arm and throwing Flynn at us. Thankfully, my reflexes hadn't deserted me, and my hand shot out, catching him before he splatted against the wall.

"Okay, okay," Doris said in a soothing voice. "Calm down. Why don't you tell us what's going on here, Denise?"

Denise began pacing, and my eyes tracked her every move, calculating the distance and effort required to take her down. I unconsciously took a step forward, and Denise swung around, arm raised toward me, in her hand… a gun.

"She's got a gun!" I squawked, shooting Doris a shocked glance, then turned my attention back to Denise. "You've got a gun."

"Well done, Sherlock," Denise sneered, but I let her sarcasm roll over me for I was still in utter shock she'd produced a weapon. I mean, I shouldn't have been surprised. This woman was capable of murder, after all, but still… a gun?

"Put the gun down, Denise. You're not going to shoot anyone," I said, keeping my cool as if I weren't staring down the barrel of a SIG 9mm.

"I could shoot you," Denise retorted, waving the pistol in an alarming manner.

"I'd rather you didn't."

Denise huffed but didn't pull the trigger.

"Why kill John?" I asked, keeping my tone conversational and light. "I mean, I can understand why you killed Seth. Heck, the whole town wanted him gone. But John? Why him?"

"He saw me."

"When? When you killed Seth?"

"Coming here." Denise's arm dropped, the gun pointing toward the floor as she ran her other hand around the back of her neck. I could practically see the cogs turning in her head, trying to figure out what to do with us. I exchanged a look with Doris who was jerking her head toward Denise. I knew what she wanted. She wanted me to take her down. Yet I hesitated. The gun was still in play, and if it went off and Doris or Flynn was hurt, I'd never forgive myself.

"Tell us about the runes," Doris said, drawing Denise's attention.

"Clever little things." Denise smiled. "No one really notices them, wouldn't think that a little rock like that could carry a death hex."

"Where did you learn how to do it? That's dark magic."

Denise shrugged. "The internet. Where else? You can learn anything on the dark web these days."

I blinked. Of course she'd learn how to perform a death spell on the internet. This was the sort of thing I'd expect from a teenager, not a woman in her seventies.

"I need to know something," Doris cut in. "Why plant Seth's bones at Holly's house?"

"To frighten her off," Denise said. "I didn't need anyone else stumbling across my setup."

"And your setup is?" I glanced behind me at the makeshift altar which was practically barren. Save for the rocks she used to hex her victims, there wasn't anything else to indicate what she'd been up to.

"I'm creating a portal. I'm becoming a member of the Shadow Binder Covenant, enabling me to bind myself to the underworld, creating a conduit for a Draughr to cross dimensions."

My mouth dropped open, and my head swung to look at Doris, who also had her jaw agape.

"Say what now?" Doris asked, aghast. "You're talking nonsense, Denise. There's no such thing as Draughrs. They're a fairytale."

"What's a Draughr?" I whispered. I'd never heard of them before.

"A hybrid. The offspring of a witch and a demon. Not real," she whispered back.

Denise's hand, the one holding the gun, swung back up. "They are real!" she cried.

"Okay, okay. Calm down," I interjected, taking a step forward. The gun turned on me.

"Why would you want to bring a Draughr here, Denise?" I wasn't really interested in her answer—the woman was clearly crazy—but my intent was to keep her talking until I could get close enough to get the gun from her. And it worked. She was ranting about the Shadowfall Amulet and the Codex of the Solstice, whatever the heck they were, while I continued inching closer. From one breath to the next, I lunged, my hands clamping around her wrist and shoving her arm straight up, the gun aimed at the ceiling.

I threw all my body weight into her, catching her off guard, so she staggered back, then her knees gave way, and we tumbled to the floor. I had a brief second of remorse about landing on top of a seventy-year-old woman, but that was quickly dashed to pieces when she punched me in the face. With my cheek throbbing, I struggled to keep hold of her, and before I knew it, Denise had thrown me to the side and was off and running, Doris hot on her heels.

"Get the gun!" I yelled. Flynn shot forward and wrapped his paws around the butt of the pistol, awkwardly dragging it across the floor. Pulling myself to my feet, I ran as fast as my injured foot would allow into the hallway, pausing to listen. Where had the women gone?

A hand clamped down on my shoulder, and without a second thought, I curled my fingers into a fist and slugged my attacker in the face.

"Ow!" Calder cursed.

"Oh. Sorry, Calder," I puffed, pinpointing footsteps overhead. I headed for the stairs, Calder right behind me.

"That's the second time you've done that." he said. "You've got good form." I waited for him to add "for a girl," but the words never came and a quick glance over my shoulder showed the grin on his face and the red mark my fist had left.

Reaching the landing, I spied Doris and Denise rolling around on the floor, wrestling. Calder moved me aside, and reaching down, he hauled Denise to her feet by her collar. Doris jumped up, keen to keep tussling. Stepping in front of her, I placed a hand on Doris's chest. "Take it easy. We've got her."

Breath heaving, Doris nodded. "Right. Good."

"You okay?" Doris's blouse was torn, and she was going to have a beauty of a black eye.

"I'm fine." She jerked her head toward Denise. "Another minute and I would have had her."

"I'm sure you would have," I consoled.

Ignoring me, Doris said to Calder, "She's the one behind Seth and John's murders. You'll find the evidence you need downstairs."

He gave me an unfathomable look, then a curt nod before marching Denise downstairs. I rounded on Doris. "How are we going to explain the runes? That Seth and John were killed by a hex? We're going to sound as crazy as Denise!"

"Didn't you ever work with local law enforcement when you were with SIA?" Doris asked, straightening her clothing. "There's an agreement of sorts."

"So, you're saying Calder does know about us after all? You said he wasn't paranormal."

"He isn't. That doesn't mean he doesn't know about us."

"Are you serious?" A surge of irritation shot through me, and I swiveled on my heel, needing some distance to get my thoughts in order.

"I'll give you a minute." Doris patted my shoulder and headed down the stairs while I stalked backward and forward on the landing.

"Uh, Holly?" Calder called.

"I'll be down in a minute!" I snapped.

"Holly, you really should—" He tried again.

"I said—" Only my words were cut off when the floor beneath me gave way. With a puff of dust and a wheeze that squeezed the last breath of air from my lungs, I landed on my back on the floor below.

Calder leaned over me, grinning. "Hey, how you doing there?"

"Yeah, good," I croaked.

"I tried to warn you."

"Shut up."

He held out his hand, and I accepted it, letting him pull me to my feet, but he didn't release his hold on my hand, instead stared into my eyes. From this range, I could see the flecks of gold in his hazel eyes and realized his lashes were equally as dark as Casey's. Why was I suddenly obsessed with eyelashes?

"Is there a single thing I can trust about you?" he asked, voice low but light.

I shook my head. "Not a thing." Honesty at last.

His lips curled into a grin before growing into a full-blown smile. "That's what I figured."

Releasing my hand, he stepped away. It wasn't until I turned to face Doris and she took one look at my face and burst out laughing that I realized anything was amiss.

"What?" I asked, touching my cheeks and hair. "What is it?"

"You're covered in dust! You look like a ghost!" Doris chortled. Even Denise had a smirk on her face. I looked down. It was true. I was covered in a layer of pale dust. Slapping at my jeans, clouds of it puffed into the air, making me cough.

"That better not trigger your allergy," Calder warned.

"It's fine." With every bone aching, I limped toward the back door. Behind me, I heard the click of handcuffs and Calder reading Denise her rights, while Doris walked sedately by my side.

"Sorry I laughed."

"That's okay."

"Are you okay? Hurt?"

"I'm fine. I'm used to bruises. How about you?" I pointed to her shiner.

She snorted. "This is nothing."

Outside, I breathed in the fresh air and waited for Calder to escort Denise out. Together, we walked back to my house.

"How did you know we were there?" I asked, jerking my head toward Reggie's house.

"Well, your place was unlocked, and the coffee was on, which meant you weren't far away. When I came around the back, I saw the trampled weeds. You left quite the trail to follow," Calder explained. "I got your message about the bones," he added.

"You know, if she hadn't left them as a way to scare me off, Seth's body might never have been found."

"Depends on if the workmen followed through and went exploring that track. And if they did a spot of break and enter when they came to the barn." He shot me a look I chose to ignore.

Flynn darted ahead of us, yellow fur resplendent in the sun. Calder's steps faltered, but he didn't reach for his gun, which I took as progress.

"Now what?" I asked no one in particular.

"She'll be charged with Seth's murder. I'm reopening John's case, although the evidence is compelling that Denise is behind his death too. Did you spot the ladder?"

I nodded. I'd seen it leaning against the back of the house.

Denise had fallen into a catatonic state, her mouth hanging slack, her eyes lacking expression. I wondered if she was preparing for an insanity plea.

Doris and I watched as he secured Denise in the back seat of his truck, gave a wave, then drove away.

Doris clapped once, then rubbed her hands together. "Let's celebrate!"

"With what? Coffee?"

"How about coffee liquor?" Doris grinned and headed inside. I followed at a slower pace. Lordy but getting beaten up by a seventy-year-old and then falling through a floor really took it out of me.

"I don't have any alcohol."

"A disastrous turn of events. One we must remedy, but don't fear, I brought some." Reaching into her handbag, she withdrew a bottle of rum, brandishing it in the air.

"You always carry rum in your bag?" I asked, sinking wearily onto a kitchen chair.

"Of course. Don't you?"

After three of the most lethal cocktails I'd ever tasted, Doris was passed out in the camp chair while I lay on the cot, praying my liver would forgive me. I could hear Flynn squeaking and sat up to watch him weave across the room.

"What's wrong with you?" I scooped him up to peer into his face, a whiff of rum and coffee reaching my nose. "Are you drunk?" I put him back on the floor, watched him stagger a little more, and laughed. "You're the worst rat I've ever had."

He looked up at me, then proceeded to vomit. Yep. Worst rat ever. Sighing, I swung my legs over the edge of the cot and headed into the kitchen for some paper towel. In the kitchen was the debris of Doris's cocktail making and the source of Flynn's current state. She'd spilled more than she'd poured, and he'd gallantly attempted to clean up behind her.

Damp paper towel was strewn around haphazardly, Doris's attempt at cleaning, I presumed. Reaching for the roll that sat on the kitchen table, I noticed a lone piece ripped from the roll and laying there, unused. Reaching for it, I froze when I noticed it had something written on it.

If you believe in legends, you should believe in curses too.

I glanced toward the living room, where Doris was still snoring her head off. Had she written it? Flynn wasn't capable of holding a pen, so it couldn't have been him. And it certainly wasn't me. Which only left

Doris. Leaving it untouched, I snatched up the roll and returned to the living room to clean up Flynn's puke. I had to admit, life hadn't been dull since moving to Gravestone, Texas.

That's the end of book one~thanks for reading!
Are you ready to continue Holly's journey in book two,
Battle of the Hexes? *Get it here:*
www.JaneHinchey.com/Gravestone/Battle of the hexes

AFTERWORD

Thank you for reading, if you enjoyed **Fur the Hex of it**, please consider leaving a review. You can find a complete list of my books, including series and reading order on my website at:

www.JaneHinchey.com

Also, if you'd like to sign up to receive emails with the latest news, exclusive offers, and more, you can do that here:

www.JaneHinchey.com/subscribe

And finally, I'd love to invite you to join my **VIP Readers group** where you get exclusive access to me, the opportunity to win one of the monthly signed paperback giveaways, join in live videos, get sneak peeks at works in progress and so much more.

www.JaneHinchey.com/LittleDevils

Thank you so much for taking a chance and reading my book - I do this for you.

xoxo

Jane

The guest list for the shifter party Kristina Gates is catering has just turned into a suspect list—for murder.

When Ted McNeil is found dead at a high society event, it looks at first like he choked on one of Kristina's cupcakes. But it soon becomes evident that foul play was involved. The cupcake was poisoned.

Kristina's determination to salvage her reputation and learn the truth launches her quest to appease the Witches' Council and avoid a life sentence in the pokey. With the help of her fae friends and sexy Watcher Ben Hoffman, she untangles a web of lies that threaten her very existence.

Faced with a mysterious foe, a family of tight-lipped shifters, and a competitor who would stop at nothing to put her out of business, Kristina realizes nothing is as it seems and the shadows hold secrets that some would kill to keep.

Get a copy of Cupcakes & Curses for FREE as a thank you for joining my newsletter! Sign up here: www.JaneHinchey.com/subscribe

About Jane

Jane Hinchey delivers snort-worthy cozy mysteries and sizzling paranormal romances that grab readers from the get-go. With tenacious heroines, lovable sidekicks, and heroes who are more than just a pretty face, her books are an irresistible mix of humor, magic, and heart. From witches cracking cases to vampires in love, she offers an adventure where the extraordinary is the norm and love bites in the best way.

Find Jane here: www.janehinchey.com

facebook.com/janehincheyauthor

instagram.com/janehincheyauthor

amazon.com/Jane-Hinchey/e/B0193449MI

bookbub.com/authors/jane-hinchey

goodreads.com/jane_hinchey

Read more by Jane

Find them all at www.JaneHinchey.com/books

The Ghost Detective Mysteries

Witch Way Paranormal Cozy Mystery Series

The Gravestone Mysteries

The Midnight Chronicles

Clean Scene Inc.

The Awakening Trilogy

Hell's Angel Trilogy

The Enforcer Series

Standalones

Returned

Secret Fates

Destiny's Touch

Blood Cursed

Heart of Darkness

www.ingramcontent.com/pod-product-compliance
Lightning Source LLC
Chambersburg PA
CBHW030753190726
48285CB00003B/832